AN AMOROUS ARRANGEMENT

Trixy thought she knew what it meant to be kissed—until the Duke of Glynde took her in his arms. Now she had learned the ecstacy of this intimacy from a master, and the Duke promised to teach her even more of pleasure—at a price.

"You're a woman of the world," he told her. "An intelligent, enterprising woman. Why, you've probably entered into the kind of arrangement I suggested before— maybe more than once."

Trixy dared not tell this smiling, supremely seductive lord that she was anything but a woman of the world.

And she feared even more to let him know what she truly was:

A woman helplessly in love . . .

MICHELLE KASEY is the pseudonym of Kasey Michaels, which is the pseudonym of Kathie Seidick, a suburban Pennsylvania native who is also a full-time wife and the mother of four children. Her love of romance, humor and history combines to make Regency novels her natural medium.

SIGNET REGENCY ROMANCE
COMING IN APRIL 1991

Carla Kelly
Libby's London Merchant

Melinda McRae
The Duke's Daughter

Gayle Buck
Mutual Consent

THE SOMERVILLE FARCE

by

Michelle Kasey

A SIGNET BOOK

SIGNET
Published by the Penguin Group
Penguin Books USA Inc., 375 Hudson Street,
New York, New York, 10014, U.S.A.
Penguin Books Ltd, 27 Wrights Lane, London W8 5TZ, England
Penguin Books Australia Ltd, Ringwood, Victoria, Australia
Penguin Books Canada Ltd, 2801 John Street,
Markham, Ontario, Canada L3R 1B4
Penguin Books (N.Z.) Ltd, 182-190 Wairau Road,
Auckland 10, New Zealand

Penguin Books Ltd, Registered Offices:
Harmondsworth, Middlesex, England

First published by Signet, an imprint of New American Library, a division of Penguin
Books USA Inc.

First Printing, March, 1991

10 9 8 7 6 5 4 3 2 1

REGISTERED TRADEMARK—MARCA REGISTRADA

PRINTED IN THE UNITED STATES OF AMERICA

BOOKS ARE AVAILABLE AT QUANTITY DISCOUNTS WHEN USED TO PROMOTE
PRODUCTS OR SERVICES. FOR INFORMATION PLEASE WRITE TO PREMIUM
MARKETING DIVISION, PENGUIN BOOKS USA INC., 375 HUDSON STREET,
NEW YORK, NEW YORK 10014.

To Nora Roberts,
who understands me—
and says she likes me anyway.

PROLOGUE

ONCE UPON A TIME in Mayfair, an insular district
snuggled within the confines of London, a mystical
place where footmen dressed like lords, where
virtue was not its own reward, and a man's wit was
measured by the height of his bank account and the
depth of his ancestors, there resided—much against
his inclination and only for as long as he deemed
necessary—a wealthy, handsome peer of the realm
christened Henry Lyle Augustus Townsend.

This gentleman, who had three years previously
ascended to the lofty station of Duke of Glynde, was
known to his contemporaries as your grace, or sir,
or, simply, Glynde, while being referred to by his
entirely unimpressed family and cronies by the
grand old English name of Harry, or Good Old
Harry, depending on the relative and Good Old
Harry's mood.

Accompanying Harry to Mayfair, or more precisely, to the Glynde mansion in Portman Square, was
his baby brother, William. Lord William, or Willie,
as he was called, was a fuzzy-cheeked, yellow-

haired, life-loving green sapling whose years numbered three months shy of twenty.

This last was not a fact with which Harry, who himself had reached the ancient age of thirty-three, was overly impressed, considering Willie's tender years to have removed his brother no more than a single step from the nursery.

In point of fact, if Harry were to have had his druthers—and considering the hey-go-mad bent of brother Willie, Harry's reluctance could be understood—the young lord would have been left behind at Glyndevaron, stoutly tied to a bedpost by his leading strings.

Accompanying Lord William, who had accompanied the duke, was a close neighbor left with the Townsends while his parents attended a house party as far from their only son as they could manage. This youth was one Mr. Andrew Carlisle, of like age and inclination as Willie; a dark-haired, sallow-complexioned, rail-thin youth who had the face and figure of a devout, impoverished assistant rector—and the heart of a dedicated prankster.

The remainder of the troupe that descended on the mansion in Portman Square included, most notably, one aunt, Lady Amelia by name—the late duke's sister. The poor lady had been married to a terribly common man by the name of Lester Fauntleroy who, instead of having the good grace to expire, leaving her a pitiable widow, had run off twenty years previously, taking a majority of Aunt Amelia's jewelry and her lady's maid with him, to live to this day in relative luxury in Jamaica. Since her sad experience, Aunt Amelia had devoted herself to the well-being of her brother's offspring, and would not have thought of remaining behind while Harry went to town.

Also in the train were the Townsend family cook, Angelo, who was Italian, a qualification that also described him, and Pinch, the treasured old family retainer—in this case, the treasured family majordomo.

There were others, of course, as no respectable peer of the realm possessing a modicum of sense travels without numerous understaff, but as they were of little import to the duke's party other than to be noticed only by their absence when the fires were left unlit or the veal arrived cold at table, they will not be mentioned here.

More to the point was the reason Glynde had chosen to travel to Mayfair in the dead of a particularly cold and messy winter, inexplicably dragging with him his nauseatingly cheerful brother, his brother's pranking bosom beau, his disheartening obtuse but lovable aunt, and creaky old Pinch. Angelo's company, on the other hand, was at least self-explanatory, as even a duke had to eat.

Simply, and not to put too fine a point on the thing, Harry had come to Mayfair to confront one slippery, difficult-to-locate Myles Somerville. Somerville—a perfect rotter of a man who three years previously, through his short-lived but profound influence over Harry's dear, daft, departed father while Harry was off somewhere fighting with Wellington—had nearly bankrupted the Townsend family.

Harry's chagrin upon discovering that his

quarry—whom he had meant with all seriousness to call out for this great crime—had just days earlier escaped London for the safer shores of Ireland, thus effectively spiking the duke's guns, or dueling pistols, was not lost upon his brother or his brother's friend.

Rather than stand by while Harry fumed, and rather than have to return to Glyndevaron to endure the remainder of a boring winter watching Harry sulk, Willie and Andy put their lamentably short-sighted heads together and devised a plan sure to make Good Old Harry the happiest man in the kingdom.

If one could not revenge oneself on the head of the household, the schemers reasoned—if, indeed, any conclusion brought forth from these two minds could be thought to have anything remotely to do with Dame Reason—why not do what was done in the "olden days," and gain that revenge through the offspring Somerville had left behind?

Yes, indeed, it seemed a kidnapping was in order! And if that offspring was female rather than male, well, wasn't that always the way of it? Harry *et al.* would hie back to Glyndevaron, the schemers would present him with their *fait accompli*, Harry would efficiently deflower the Somerville chit, and then he would send her back to her reprobate father, head bowed and spirit broken, a mere shell of her former gloriously beautiful, chaste self.

Or, even better, Harry would fall in love with the chit, who most probably was totally unlike her father, but rather a diamond of the first water who had the heart of an angel. Harry would then exchange his wearying passion for revenge for an equally consuming passion for the daughter of his old enemy—leaving Willie and Andy a lot more freedom to do as they pleased—and everyone would be the happier for it.

Truly, it was a most beautiful revenge, a wondrously brilliant, flawless plan that benefited everyone concerned; something straight out of all those glorious stories of knights of old.

However, if the Somerville offspring turned out to be plural rather than singular, and if that offspring came most inconveniently equipped with both maid and governess—who would put up an awful racket at being left behind, queering the whole idea at the outset—that just might present a wee problem.

But these were minor considerations, piddling details barely worth fretting about. Most important was the revenge—and the dash and thrill of the thing. Willie and Andy had their job to do, and they would do it; a brilliant job of work for which any brother so depressed by his inability to arrange his own revenge would be endlessly grateful.

After all, Good Old Harry was the smart one. He wouldn't have any trouble figuring out what to do with the excess hostages—would he?

1

"LORD LOVE A DUCK, Willie, d'ya have to make all that racket? What is that, anyway? You sound like you dragged half a blacksmith's shop along with us."

Lord William uncurled himself from the crouch he had taken up behind his friend and opened his cloak, the light from a nearby streetlamp—one of the few lining the street and a more inconveniently located structure no one could imagine—shining on a collection of knives, mallets, and a particularly sinister-looking metal bar, the whole of it tied around his neck by way of lengths of rope. "D'ya like 'em, Andy? The bar is to force open the lady's window, the ropes are to tie her up with, and the knives are for fighting our way out with her if she screams."

"And what's the mallet for?" Andy inquired, much impressed with his friend's foresight as well as his bloodthirsty inclinations. "You aren't going to tap her over the head, are you? It doesn't seem sporting. I mean, we are two against one, and the one's female into the bargain."

Hunkering down again, the two of them having taken up places behind a large rain barrel located on the side of the Somervilles' small rented house in Half Moon Street, Willie explained that the mallet was for hitting anyone he didn't think deserved skewering. "Anyone like Pinch, for instance," he whispered as one of the watch was passing by the end of the alley. "I don't think I'd have the heart for sticking a Pinch, do you?"

Andy reached back to ruffle Willie's gold curls as his friend made a pained face at the thought of harming the Glynde family butler. "I don't think you have the stomach for it either," he said, grinning, his smile splitting his long, thin face and lending a slight sparkle to his dark, hedgehog eyes. "Now, pay attention. That's twice the charlie has gone past. If my calculations are correct, he won't be back this way for at least an hour. That should give us plenty of time to do what we have to do."

"It bloody well better, Andy," Willie warned, rising to jump up on top of the barrel. "It'll be dawn in another three hours and Harry said we're leaving for Glyndevaron at first light. Any later than that and he'll be sure to notice that we've added to the parade of coaches hired for the trip out of London." Holding on to a convenient ledge, he hoisted himself up onto the closest balcony and held out an arm to his friend. "Here—up you go, Andy."

Andy, whose spirit might be in the right place, but whose stomach and heart were decidedly opposed to heights, hesitated a moment before allowing

Willie to pull him up alongside him onto the balcony, a rickety wrought-iron appendage to the building that seemed to remain in place more by luck than engineering.

"Get out that bar," Andy whispered hastily, clinging to the rough, crumbly brick with all his stength, refusing to look down. "See if you can use it to pry open the window. Hurry, Willie, I don't like the feel of this balcony. It seems to be moving under my feet."

Convinced that the balcony was sturdy, aware of his friend's dislike for heights, and not averse to having a little fun with the fellow, Willie shook his head, stating firmly that he was sure the Somerville girl's bedroom could not be located on this floor.

"And don't be so missish, Andy," he admonished. "The balcony's fine. Look—I'll prove it." So saying, he jumped up and down three times, his small arsenal of weapons jingling with his every movement—while the balcony continued to sway and creak for a full three seconds after he had stopped his assault on it. "There. Are you happy now? Lord knows I am," he said, turning his head to hide his grin.

Andy, his abused fingertips all but burrowing into the crumbling brick, glared at his friend through the darkness. "You did that on purpose, Willie," he declared feelingly.

"Well, of course I did. You knew that. And to think that you're the one who told me a gentleman never points out the obvious. For shame, Andy. I say, Andy, you're looking pale in the moonlight. Do you feel all right? I tell you, it's hard to believe this was all your idea. But to return to what I said before about the location of Miss Somerville's bed-chamber: I think we should climb that drain over there—it leads up to the next balcony."

Not caring that they might be found out, hauled off to the guardhouse, and then rescued from jail only to be read a blistering scold by the duke, Andy gritted loudly: "Willie, open that damned window! Now!"

"Why don't you shout a little louder, Andy, and the whole place might come tumbling down—like that Joshua fellow, you know?" Willie suggested, unearthing the bar and setting to with a will, working to pry open the window. Fun was fun, but it was time they were moving on.

"Well, isn't that depressing?" he remarked a moment later in disgust as the window slid up silently. "The fool thing wasn't even locked. You have to wonder, Andy, what this world is coming to when people don't even bother to lock their own windows. It's inviting trouble, that's what it is. Just think about it a minute, Andy. Anybody at all could have come here tonight and robbed them blind— or worse. Anybody at all!"

"Oh, shut up, Willie," Andy ordered, rudely shoving his friend to one side before—with a remarkable lack of grace—he launched himself headlong into the Somerville town house. Graceless maneuvers tending to result in equally graceless landings, there came almost immediately the loud crash of breaking glass, followed by an equally loud masculine curse and a single piercing female scream, then the sickening thud of Andy's body making rude contact with the wooden floor, and, lastly, the anguished voice of a woman—obviously Irish—calling upon the dearest Virgin Mary and all the saints to protect her poor babies from being murdered in their beds.

Now, Willie might have agreed with Andy that Adventure, if not his middle name, was at least on speaking terms with him, but the chaos taking place in the dark on the other side of the half-open window did not immediately seem to him to fit his description of Adventure. Other, less pleasing words came more readily to mind; words like Disaster, or Mayhem, or Incarceration, or—worst of all—Harry.

He had a choice to make, and he had to make it quickly. He could either dive into the town house to rescue his friend, who—by the sounds he heard filtering out to him—was at that moment being struck heavily about the head and shoulders with some article of furniture, or he could scamper back down the way he had come, join a cavalry regiment under an assumed name, and hope for a quick, relatively painless death at the hands of any leftover enemy of England he could find to do the deed.

The fact that it was nearing the end of the quarter and he had barely enough allowance left to him to buy a meat pie on the corner, let alone a commission; the knowledge that he was just now entering the prime of his life and to date had not even so much as talked to an opera dancer, so that he had no real desire to die for his country—or anyone else, for that matter; and the niggling suspicion that Andy would at some later date discover him wherever he might hide and strip off all his skin inch by inch, toughened Willie's resolve, so that, after taking a deep, steadying breath, he ducked his head and stepped through the window.

The scene that met his eyes, regrettably only partially lit by the small brace of candles sitting to one side of the room, was not without humor. Andy, never stout, was still on the floor on his back, reminding Willie of an overturned sea turtle he had once seen on the beach at Brighton, his hands and feet all raised to protect himself. Hovering over Andy, armed only with an evil-looking embroidery tambour frame, which she was wielding with a vengeance, stood a very small, yet truly enormous woman of indeterminate years, her heavy white cotton ruffled nightgown billowing about her like a man-o'-war in full sail.

Reaching under his cloak, Willie pulled out a length of rope, took another measuring look at the woman's girth, and extracted a second length.

"Ye filthy, nasty divil, ye," the woman, who was so intent on her victim that she had not noticed Willie's presence, was saying in a low growling brogue, every other word punctuated by a swing of the tambour frame, "Oi'll not be surrenderin' me vir-ture ta the loiks o' ye!"

"Vir*tue*, ma'am," Willie corrected, coming up behind her to tap lightly on her shoulder. "The word is 'virtue.' Now, leave off, do, before you hurt the poor fellow."

The woman swung about, nearly clipping Willie on the ear with the frame before he could throw one rope over her back and, together, they fell to the floor—landing atop the already beleaguered Andy, who was still trying to catch his breath.

A moment later, his hands full wrestling with the woman as the two of them rolled over and over across the floor, knocking down small tables and scattering knickknacks pell-mell all over the place, Willie called out frantically for Andy to lend him a hand—preferably both hands—before the woman's bulk crushed the life out of him.

Another man, seeing the seriousness of the situation, and weighing the chances that the Somerville chit would hear the commotion and summon aid— which was sure to bode ill for the two house-breakers—would have immediately set to with a will, assisting his friend by employing the piece of rope lying at his feet, using it to at least tie the woman's fat, flailing ankles together.

But then, another man hadn't just been all but frightened into disgracing himself by a person who, by the by, was supposed to be his most particular *bon ami,* who had jumped up and down on a rickety balcony—in unholy glee, it must be added—when that second person had known that the first person might just end by tossing up his supper.

"I wouldn't dream of interfering, my good friend," he pronounced evenly as Willie once more pleaded with him for assistance. "You seem to be doing splendidly on your own. There are only two of you rolling around down there, aren't there? Strange, but you appear to be a crowd."

Leaning against the table he had so lately made acquaintance with in a much ruder manner as he landed on it nose-first upon entering the room, Andy crossed one ankle over the other, produced a wide, closed-mouth grin, and watched his friend in action. "Will you use the knife or the mallet, dear boy?" he asked conversationally a few moments later as he saw Willie struggling to reach his store of weapons. "She's more a Pound than a Pinch, you know."

Willie's next exchange with his friend was not only unquotable but unprintable as well, although it did elicit a sharp bark of laughter from Andy, who had at last decided that his revenge was complete and slowly bent to retrieve the second length of rope before, with the two of them working together, they at last succeeded in tying up the woman.

A few perspiration-producing moments later, Andy's handkerchief stuck in her mouth, the woman—whose hopes, fears, inclination, or assessment of her charms was much greater than that of the two boys—was left trussed up nearly head to foot to lie in the middle of the floor, her wide blue eyes staring up at what, to her, must have looked to be the soon-to-be possessors of her "vir-ture."

"There," Andy said, straightening his disheveled clothing after tying the last knot, "that has her all right and tight. I told you it would be easy. Shall we now proceed to Miss Somerville's bed-chamber?"

Andy's statement seemed to breathe new life into the trussed-up woman, who had been lying quite still— whether stoically awaiting or eagerly antici-pating her fate, only she knew—and she began to throw her body from side to side as unintelligible sounds emanated from her handkerchief-muzzled mouth.

Willie looked down at the woman, his young heart

stung by her distress, and he hastened to explain. "You would be Miss Somerville's maid, I suppose. No, please don't try to answer. I'm convinced you must be. Well, madam, there is no need to fret. We're just here to abduct your charge and take her to m'brother—so he can ravish her, you understand. But he's a duke, so maybe he'll fall in love with her and we'll all have a happy ending—even though it doesn't look too good right now, does it?"

"Well, that certainly served to ease her mind," Andy remarked sarcastically, watching as the rotund maid's blue eyes all but popped from her fat, pudding cheeks and her struggles to free herself increased tenfold. "You told her about the duke, you know. Why don't you gift her with his name as well? That way the constable won't have to bother hying back and forth up and down the countryside looking for us among all the dukes."

Willie looked positively stricken. He slapped one palm against his forehead, cursing himself for his big mouth, before inspiration struck him with even more force. "That's no problem, Andy. We'll simply take the maid along with us. That way there'll be no one left here to give the alarm."

Andy looked assessingly at the maid's still-squirming bulk and then at his long, stringy arms. "Who carries her to the coach?" he asked, considering the plan.

"We both carry her," Willie declared emphatically, settling the matter. "There are two flights of stairs to consider, you know, and I still harbor some faint hopes of one day siring children. Now, come on. Let's find the girl and get out of here. The coach will be outside soon."

Over the maid's fervent but muffled protests, the pair went on the hunt for the staircase and ascended to the next floor of the tall, narrow house. With Andy shushing Willie, whose remaining store of tools was clanking together beneath his cloak, they crept stealthily down the hall, to stop outside the door Andy had selected as being the one of the three on the floor that seemed to him most likely to contain Miss Somerville.

Seeing no light peeping out from beneath the door —and, truly, why should there be, as it was past four in the morning and no respectable young miss would have a reason to burn her candle past two, even in the midst of the Season—Willie grasped the bent metal handle and pushed down.

There came a quiet "click," followed by a slight squeak as the door swung open into the darkened chamber. Stuck so close together as to appear joined at the hip, the two plotters tiptoed into the room, their backs bent nearly in half, their eyes darting back and forth as they searched through the gloom for the bed.

And, lo and behold, there it was, nearly straight in front of them, a large bed piled high with comforters and pillows, lying among which lay, not one, but two young ladies.

Andy looked at Willie. Willie looked back at Andy. Their brows rose, to hang suspended high above their wide, perplexed eyes. Their lips formed the word "Two?" Their heads turned once more toward the bed, then swiveled back to each other. "Two?"

Andy, decidedly the more adventuresome of *their* particular "two"—as long as both feet were planted firmly on the ground—ventured around one side of the bed and looked down on the two sleeping faces. Wordlessly he pointed to two heads crowned by glorious guinea-gold hair, then two identically shaped faces—or profiles, as those were all that were visible.

He tiptoed back to the bottom of the bed. "It's like looking into a mirror," he said, awed.

Willie rolled his eyes. "Don't be stupid, Andy. It's nothing like looking in a mirror. If you looked in a mirror, you'd see yourself. But I know what you mean. I can see two girls—very lovely girls, too. Twins, I'm sure. Which one do we take, do you think?"

Andy frowned, considering the question. "The elder? But how would we know? The prettier? They're as alike as peas in a pod. Perhaps we should toss a coin and have done with it. Dash me, I hadn't counted on two of them."

Willie, who had already come to a decision— enjoying this temporary position of power over his nonplussed compatriot—shook his head decisively. "Toss a coin? We take them both, you nodcock. Think about it. We're already lugging the maid along to keep her silent. We can't leave one of 'em behind to do what we won't let the maid do. Besides, look at them, Andy. They look so helpless. What would one do without the other? No," he said, reaching into the voluminous pockets of his cloak for the sack he had brought to stuff the Somerville chit in, "we take them both. You take the one on the right, and I'll take the other. Quickly, now."

Left without a sack, and with Willie already on the move, Andy swallowed hard and approached the head of the bed, his hands held in front of him, not knowing precisely where to place them. In the end, he decided on the young girl's shoulders, which were barely visible above the coverlet.

It proved to be an unfortunate choice. While Willie's twin struggled, her screams muffled beneath the heavy cloth of the sack, Andy's twin was left with her mouth free. Her eyes opened wide in shock, she employed her voice to good effect, screaming so loudly into Andy's nearby ear that he suffered a momentary qualm that he might have been rendered deaf as a lamppost.

"For the love of heaven, Andy, shut her up!" Willie commanded, tying a length of rope around the edges of the sack that reached to the young girl's knees before hefting her, kicking wildly, onto his shoulder. "Yours is screaming fair to raise the dead."

"Hardly, sirrah," came a tightly controlled female voice from the doorway. "But Eugenie's cry for help has fortunately succeeded in summoning me."

The boys whirled about in surprise, Willie's burden all but slipping over his shoulder onto the floor before he regained his senses enough to grab onto a pair of bare, shapely ankles. "Who . . . who are you?"

Eugenie, the screamer, had been immediately released by the audibly abused Andy, who had passed the point of caring much one way or the other how the night ended, just as long as it did.

"Trixy!" Eugenie shrieked, causing Andy once more to grab at his ear, "we're being abducted. It's just like that book Helena and I read last week, the one from the lending library. I'm quite assured we're being abducted."

"And I'm equally assured that you are not being abducted," the woman she had addressed as Trixy answered calmly, the reason for this assurance gleaming dully in the faint light coming in from the streetlamp located outside the window. Motioning with the barrel of the evil-looking pistol, she commanded softly, "If you gentlemen would kindly step against the wall—after you have redeposited Miss Helena Somerville on the bed and untied her—perhaps we can discuss what is to be done now."

Lord William stubbornly remained stock-still as Miss Helena Somerville's wiggling bare toes tickled at his nose.

"Willie, for God's sake, put her down," Andy pleaded, his hands raised high above his head. A pistol was to be respected, Andy knew, but that same pistol in the hands of a woman was to be feared. "It's over. We've botched it."

2

THE DUKE OF GLYNDE was pleased to be home, even if his trip to London had proved frustratingly unprofitable. Myles Somerville still lived, a thought that galled the duke's eye-for-eye sense of right and wrong even as the realization that he himself, not having become a killer on the field of honor, would be allowed to continue living unfettered on his beloved Glyndevaron estate, rather than being forced to flee to the Continent in order to escape the long arm of the king's justice.

Glynde was not by nature a violent man, and although he had more than once distinguished himself by his bravery in battle on the Peninsula, he much preferred to be remembered as a commander who had cared first and foremost for the safety and well-being of the men in his command.

It was only since the death of his father that Harry had realized that it was one thing to care for the soldiers dependent upon him in wartime, and quite another to be responsible for his brother,

William, a young man whose reckless *joie de vivre* was enough to turn the head of the bravest of men white overnight.

The thought of what havoc William, left on his own, would cause to the family name if the duke ended by spilling his claret on the dueling ground, had kept Harry from racing off all alone to the city in pursuit of Myles Somerville the moment he had learned the man had taken up residence in London in preparation for the Season.

In the end, he had taken William with him—William and his reprobate friend, Andrew—if only to have the boy close at hand in case the unthinkable should happen. That way, Harry had reasoned, the family solicitors should not have to first bail William out of some country jail before informing him that he had become the twelfth duke.

He had not, he realized now, considered the possibility that William, engulfed in the throes of grief, might immediately challenge Somerville to yet another duel, in order to avenge both his father and his brother. Harry thought of it now, trying in vain to picture a stony-eyed William staring down the barrel of a pistol at his opponent.

The mental image dissolved nearly as quickly as it formed. No, William would never do such a thing. The boy would seek revenge, Harry was convinced of that—for William did love him—but it wouldn't be a conventional revenge. William had made it a point never, ever, to submit to the conventional if a more dashing, inventive plan would serve as well.

Yet, Harry reasoned, pacing the length of his study, William had behaved most properly for the week they had remained in London and, surprisingly, had seemed all but overjoyed to be returning to Glyndevaron without partaking in any of the varied and ribald activities the metropolis had to offer.

Harry frowned, his steps leading him to a window, where he stood looking out on the west lawn. Why did William's good behavior gnaw on the edges of his brain? The explanation came quickly: it bothered Harry because it wasn't normal. It wasn't natural for William to be good, it wasn't expected.

What it was, as a matter of fact, was deucedly unnerving. It wasn't like William not to be running some rig, existing in, or on the precipice of, some sort of trouble. Having a well-behaved William around was much like having a lighted bomb tucked inside one's pants—not only extremely uncomfortable but also deadly.

Harry stood at the window for some time, his hands clasped behind his back, the afternoon sun glinting dully on his dark hair and highlighting his clear, chiseled profile. He frowned once or twice, remembering both his failed revenge and his brother's seeming bid for a halo, both remembrances jabbing at him like small needles, keeping him from enjoying the usually pleasing scene outside the window.

Perhaps, he thought, shrugging, he was overtired from spending eight long hours on the road, traveling back to Glyndevaron, the trip following hard on a nearly sleepless week spent on a fruitless hunt across London for Somerville. That could explain the niggling feeling that something wasn't right.

It could, he mused further, conjuring up yet another mental picture of his brother's rather woe-begone face as they had climbed the steps to Glyndevaron a scant half-hour ago—but he most seriously doubted it.

"Ah, there you are, Harry. We've been looking for you."

Glynde slowly turned on his heels to stand, the sun at his back, watching as William and Andrew edged hesitantly into the study. "William . . . Andrew," he said wearily, inclining his head. "You boys aren't wearing your usual happy, smiling faces. Might I assume you aren't overjoyed with our precipitate return to Glyndevaron?" he asked, something inside him making him probe for some slight hint that might explain his growing feeling that the "bomb" in his clothing was burning down closer to the end of its fuse. "Perhaps you didn't get to see every dark den of iniquity in London but, I assure you, they will still be there waiting for you when we return to the city in April."

"Oh, cut line, Harry!" Willie protested, throwing himself into a nearby chair. "You know as well as I do that Andy and I didn't so much as knock over a charlie's box or roll a single pair of dice in any gaming hell for the entirety of the time we were in town. It was quite dashed dull, as a matter of fact—almost the whole week."

"Almost?" Harry questioned, his instincts—and the pinched look on Andy's thin face—urging him to delve deeper. "Then I may relax, William, knowing that you did discover some small amusement to take your mind off the thought that your beloved brother might be leaving the house at any moment either to kill or to be killed?"

Willie gave a careless wave of his hand. "Oh, that," he said dismissively. "There was never any danger of you dying, Harry. All the world knows what a splendid shot you are—and what a marvel you are with a sword. We never gave a second thought to your chances for dispatching Somerville without so much as breaking a sweat."

"How very gratifying—I think," Glynde pronounced ruefully, wondering how he had ever thought William might have gained his solemn expression from worry about his safety.

Andrew, prudently taking up an easily defensible position behind William's chair, his long fingers kneading the burgundy leather of the chair back, piped up, "It was only when you discovered that Somerville had flown the coop that poor devoted Willie here became distressed." He leaned forward, looking down at William even as one long finger poked his friend in the neck. "Ain't that right, Willie?"

Willie, slapping Andy's jabbing finger away, responded quickly, "Right, Andy. Right as rain. Powerfully distressed I was, to see m'brother thwarted in his bid for revenge."

"Not revenge, William, at least not to my mind. Justice, I'd call it," Harry slid in, his sharp dark eyes not missing Andy's urgent poke or William's testy response. "Myles Somerville bilked our trusting father out of half a fortune, and the humiliation of the thing hastened Papa's death. No matter that I've managed to recoup our losses and more, the principle of the thing remains."

"Um, precisely," Willie agreed, nodding. "I'm a firm believer in principles m'self, as a matter of fact. I am, ain't I, Andy?" he asked, pushing back his head to look up at his friend. "It can really set me off—just to think about the principle of the thing."

"Willie's a real firebrand," Andy agreed immediately, looking at Glynde. "That's why I couldn't stop him when he decided to take matters into his own hands."

"What!" Willie leapt from the chair to turn and glare at this traitor to some yet unknown, nebulous situation Harry was increasingly seeing as "the burning fuse." Willie took two steps forward, and Andy took three back. "What do you mean, 'he decided to take matters into his own hands'? You were the one that was prattling nineteen to the dozen about knights of old and blood feuds and all that rot. You were the one that said it would be as simple as spitting in a puddle. You were the one that said Harry would be tickled to death 'to do the dirty deed.' You were the one that—"

"Yes, one! One, I said!" Andy interrupted, holding up a single finger and wagging it in Willie's face. "I said it would work with one. I never said anything about more than that, now, did I? Think on it, Willie. One was all I mentioned. I thought we could count on your brother for one. I never said he was a bloody stallion."

"Oh, really? Well, who was it who said it didn't

make any never-mind, huh?" Willie challenged, advancing yet another step. "And who was it who couldn't come up with a single idea to get us out of the mess you got us into—you, who are always so brimful with marvelous ideas? Answer me that, will you?"

"Boys," Harry said, interposing himself between his brother and Andy before the boys could come to actual blows. He had seen the two friends come to physical violence before, and it wasn't easy to intervene once the fisticuffs had begun.

As a matter of fact, following one memorable occasion upon which Harry had ended up with an inadvertent black eye, delivered by one of the combatants, he had taken to throwing a bucket of water on them as they rolled about on the floor, flailing at each other. It was messy, and terribly hard on the carpets if the contretemps took place indoors, the duke had acknowledged when Pinch showed signs of taking exception to the procedure, but it was eminently less personally painful to Harry.

"I think we'd best have a small talk, boys," he said now. "What is all this business about knights of old—and why would I need to be a stallion? I have to tell you, I don't much like the sound of this. Now, what foolish mess have you two created this time?"

Willie—his weight pressing hard against his brother's palm, which was at that moment pressed against the younger man's chest as that same young man leaned forward, the better to reach his opponent—narrowed his eyes to say exasperatedly, forgetting that this small particle of information had yet to be shared with his sibling, "It's that terrible woman, of course. What else could be the problem?"

"Just the one woman? What about the others?" Andy said by way of rebuttal, leaning against the duke's other palm, his hands reaching forward on the off-chance he might be able to get in at least one good shot at his fellow conniver. "I should think you'd believe the others to be a small bit of the problem. Especially the last one. She's the one what queered the whole thing."

The Duke of Glynde, suppressing a suddenly happier memory of days spent battling biting insects and debilitating heat on the Peninsula while on the lookout for enemy snipers in the hills, took two fistfuls of shirt—one in either hand—and pulled the two arguing youths to within a flea's whisker of his own face. "From the beginning, boys—now!" he commanded tersely, his dark eyes flashing fire.

So saying, and after shifting his narrowed gaze first to one boy, then the other, Harry pushed them both rudely away and sat down in the chair William had recently vacated. "I'm waiting, boys. It has, all in all, been a trying week. Don't push my patience beyond another moment."

Willie and Andy, who had only seconds earlier believed there could be no greater joy in life than that of beating each other senseless, exchanged glances, immediately called a silent truce, and joined forces against a common enemy. Arms linked, they stepped in front of the chair, prepared to make a clean breast of things.

"I . . ." Andy began, and then as Willie pointedly

cleared his throat, amended, "that is, we—Willie and I—were very worried about your distressed state when you learned that Somerville had flown the coop."

Willie nodded vigorously. "Terribly worried, Harry. You could have gone into a decline or taken up gambling or something, for all we knew. It didn't seem fair."

"So, knowing you'd have to return to Glyndevaron without having the chance to put a ball or a poke into Somerville, we decided that you might be able to revenge yourself in some other way."

Andy leered at his friend. "Yes, Willie wanted ... I mean, we wanted you to be able to poke somebody, right?"

Willie, who hadn't blushed in years, turned beet red from his chin to the roots of his blond hair.

Harry closed his eyes as the fuse burned down closer to the bomb, lighting a small fire in his belly. "Go on," he urged quietly, the words "knights of old" ringing in his ears. Had the two nodcocks actually believed he would ... ? No, it was impossible, even for them.

When the boys hesitated, he added, still with his eyes shut, "Perhaps it might help move things along a trifle if I tell you that I am aware Somerville has two daughters."

Andy's thin, underpaid-assistant-rector's solemn face split into an unholy grin. "Oh, yes, sir, that does help, indeed. Did you know they are twins—the daughters, I mean? Sleep in the same bed and everything?"

Glynde's eyes popped open and he impaled Andy with their hot glare. "And just how did you come by that interesting piece of information, Mr. Carlisle?" he asked tightly. "To this moment, I had foolishly assumed you two were lamenting the failure of what I'm sure, in your minuscule minds, you perceived to be a brilliant plan. Are you trying to tell me you actually took your lunacy so far as to succeed in gaining access to Miss Somerville's bedchamber?"

"The Misses Somerville," Willie stated punctiliously, stepping forward a pace to help bring home his point. "There are two of 'em, Harry, remember?"

"How silly of me to forget," Glynde responded, something in his tone causing Willie to beat a hasty retreat, and he rejoined Andrew, the two of them all but clinging together for, obviously, they were about to come to the crux of the story.

"Yes, well, sir," Andy said, running a fingertip beneath his suddenly too-tight collar, "it is important, I suppose, to remember that there were—are—two of them. That makes four, altogether."

"Four *what* altogether?" the duke asked, unable to understand. "Four women you threw into high hysterics? Four women who are, even as we speak, laying charges against you in London? Four women whose throats you slit to gain their silence? Four women who . . . Good God, now I'm thinking like the pair of you!"

"Just four altogether, Harry," Willie added, his courage reviving as he saw his brother's anger begin to crumble into incomprehensibility. "The girls—they're twins, you remember; you seem to keep forgetting that, and it's quite important, actually—the maid, and that terrible governess woman. She's the worst of them. Everything would have been fine—even if Miss Somerville being twins had thrown a kink into our plans—if it just hadn't been for her."

Still, like Willie, smarting from his treatment at the hands of the Somerville governess, Andy burst into speech. "I still say we could have scraped through with the maid and the girls. If only that dratted female hadn't had the pistol."

Grown men shouldn't cry, Harry knew, but there were times when it seemed the only alternative to physical mayhem. "William!" he commanded, rising to place himself directly in front of his trembling brother. "I demand you tell me what you did to Miss Somerville—either one or both Misses Somerville—and I demand that you tell me now."

As Willie opened his mouth to speak, Harry held out a hand to silence him until he finished laying down the conditions of the confession. "But, William, before you say anything, think: if you are about to tell me that now, at this moment, there are two hysterical young girls waiting upstairs in my bed, ready for me to enact some Middle Ages revenge on their undoubtedly chaste bodies, I shall most probably murder you!"

"Well, of course not!" Willie exploded in exasperation, shaking his head. "Why would I do a thing like that? Two of 'em in your bed—and at one and the same time? I should hardly think so, even for you. Don't talk nonsense, Harry."

Harry allowed his chin to sink onto his chest.

"Thank God," he murmured, relieved. For a moment there he had actually begun to believe his brother had been idiotic enough to kidnap the Somerville twins and bring them to Glyndevaron for him to deflower.

He should have known better. William and his maggoty friend had probably gone so far as to climb a drain and peep in on the girls—that much folly he could easily lay at their doorsteps—but even William was too intelligent to actually carry out such a harebrained scheme.

"No," Andy corrected happily—just as the duke remembered something about there being two other women, and a pistol that seemed to figure heavily somewhere in the story—"we wouldn't do anything half so shabby. They're upstairs in the west wing, all tucked up nice and tight."

The bomb finally exploded. "You did *what*? They're tucked up *where*?" Harry shouted, his head shooting up so quickly he thought he heard a small snap at his nape. "Willie, you didn't?" He grabbed his brother on either side of his neck, shaking him until the younger man's teeth rattled audibly. "For the love of heaven, Willie, tell me you didn't!"

Willie raised his hands to pry his brother's fingers away from his Adam's apple. "I . . . we . . . that is, damn it, Andy, help me!"

"There's no need to choke the information out of him, your grace," interrupted a female voice from the doorway. "I should be more than happy to take the explanation from here as, at the rate they are progressing now, it will be years before they've finished."

Harry, his hands stilled in the act of throttling

William, looked past his brother to see a tall, slim red-haired woman past her first blush of youth standing just inside the study, her arms folded neatly at her waist.

"Who in bloody hell are you?" he asked, his usual good manners having somehow become a casualty of his brother's exploding bomb. "And how the devil did you get here?"

"We added another traveling coach at the end of the coaches we used coming back from town," Andy supplied quickly, feeling much braver with a woman in the room, as the duke wasn't likely to commit murder in front of a witness—and most especially this particular witness, who had the most disturbing way of turning another person's misfortune to her own advantage. Besides, if his grace was going to wreak violence on anybody, it appeared William had been elected as the most immediate target.

"Mmm-mmfffh!" Willie gurgled unintelligibly, still vainly clawing at his brother's stilled, yet nevertheless tightly gripping hands.

"It all seemed easy enough," Andy hastened to add before his courage deserted him, "what with you riding up front in the lead coach. We figured you'd never notice another one tagging along behind, especially as we had packed them a lunch so that they didn't have to eat with us and told the coachman to drive directly to the stables, while you were let off at the front door. And you didn't. Notice anything, that is. Only there wasn't supposed to be anyone in the coach save Miss Somerville—save one Miss Somerville."

The duke ignored the youth to continue staring

at the red-haired woman, who was now walking about the room idly inspecting the bookshelves. "I repeat, ma'am—who are you?"

"I am Beatrice Stourbridge—known to my charges as Trixy, a truly horrible name, almost as horrible as Beatrice. I have been, over the past several years, variously employed as governess, companion, and general drudge, forced to earn my living by squiring about young girls whose main purpose in life is, it seems, to torture me with their inanity. You don't know me, but I have heard of you—and your dislike for my employer, for which I can only commend you, as Mr. Somerville is a truly odious man. You may not know this, your grace, but you are to be my salvation, my release from the drudgery of ape-leading simpering misses until I am so frayed and worn I slip, unlamented, into an early grave. Isn't that right, boys?"

Harry slid his bemused gaze from Miss Beatrice Stourbridge to his brother, belatedly realizing that he had been all but choking the life out of the young scamp. He let his hands fall limply to his sides. "Don't say another word, William—just let me hazard a guess. She's the one with the pistol, right?"

3

ANDY, WHO HAD BEEN QUIET much longer than was his custom, stepped forward to take up the story. "She had the twins tie us up while, right on the spot, she thought up the most terrible scheme you can imagine." He leaned close to the duke to whisper in the man's ear, "I don't think she's a real lady, your grace. Her mind's as sharp as a tack—her tongue too."

"What is this scheme, Andrew?" the duke whispered back, still looking at Miss Stourbridge, who seemed to have lost interest in the conversation, as she was showing all the outward signs of being engrossed in a volume of Plato. "How did she force you to bring her here?"

Andy rolled his eyes at the man, obviously wondering how a supposedly bright man like the duke could ask such a silly question. "She had the pistol—that's how. Remember?"

There was a short tinkling laugh, uttered by Miss Stourbridge, who could not have been as engrossed in Plato as Harry had believed. "How do you stand them, your grace?" she asked, smiling. "I imagine it will be easier for me to tell you the whole of it. To reiterate, Mr. Myles Somerville is not, forgive me, a nice man. He deserted his twins—within minutes of hearing about your arrival in town—and without making any plans to reclaim them ever again. He left us with two full months' rent owing on the town house, not a copper penny in the house, and no prospects. Yet, just as I was at my wits' end, your brother and his friend showed up to save the day. It's simple, and, I must say, rather brilliant—my plan, that is."

Harry looked at the woman through narrowed eyes. "Go on," he said smoothly, reaching out to hold his brother's elbow, as the youth was showing signs of wilting to the floor.

"My plan, your grace? As I have already said, it is really quite simple. For my silence in the matter, you shall provide me with a way out of my personal dilemma, your grace, by gifting me with a small, modest cottage somewhere near the sea—I've always enjoyed the seaside—as well as a comfortable but not overly ambitious allowance with which to support myself.

"I shall, thanks to you and your brother, be free to live out the rest of my life in some peace of mind, never fearing that one of my inane charges will someday lead me to committing mayhem—either on my charge or on myself, I will not dare to conjecture. However, as I have, against my own good judgment I assure you, grown rather fond of Eugenie and Helena, I cannot in good conscience abandon them and still rejoice in my own good fortune."

"She says they'll end up making their living on their backs otherwise," Willie put in quietly. "Well, don't look at me like that, Harry—she's the one that said it!"

"If I might continue?" Miss Stourbridge replaced the book on the shelf and walked over to join the gentlemen. "The girls will have to be settled, your grace, before my mind can be made easy. That's where you come in—again."

Glynde pulled himself up to his full imposing height and glared down at his aristocratic nose at Miss Stourbridge. "I can't see how, madam," he intoned icily. "As a matter of fact, I can't see where I figure in any of your greedy, overly ambitious plans."

She smiled, showing her even white teeth. "Can't you, your grace? I should have thought it was obvious. Your brother tried to kidnap two innocent young girls so that you could have your pick of which one to ravish in order to revenge yourself on their father." She shook her head. "That wasn't nice, your grace. It wasn't nice at all. As a matter of fact, I daresay it was downright criminal."

The right side of Harry's mouth lifted in a wry smile. "But—for a price—you, I gather, won't tell anybody. That, for want of a better word, is blackmail, Miss Stourbridge."

She smiled again. "Yes, your grace, it is. How good of you to point that out to me. It is not, however, kidnap and ravishment, is it? Those are much worse crimes, both legally and in the court of opinion—in society. I pointed that out to your brother and his friend, and they were quick to agree."

"At which point, Miss Stourbridge, they gathered up you and the twins and brought you all here, to Glyndevaron, so that I could pay you off."

"Don't forget the maid, Harry," Willie added. "She's Irish, and ever so fat. We had to bring her too, or else Eugenie wouldn't come. She even cried—Eugenie did—when we said we wanted to leave the dratted woman behind."

"Eugenie is extremely attached to Lacy," Miss Stourbridge corroborated, wincing slightly. "As a matter of fact, Eugenie is quite attached to a multitude of things—a most loving, devoted, caring child. Perhaps you shall wish to concentrate on Helena instead. She's not nearly so quick, but she's an amenable-enough little wigeon."

Harry was confused. He thought he had been handed a problem that could be settled with the simple application of money. "Why should I have anything to do with either of them beyond gifting them with a few hundred pounds?" he asked, hating himself for having to voice the question.

Miss Stourbridge smiled yet again, and Glynde realized he was fast becoming very disenchanted with the woman's smile, as it smacked of condescension. "Why, your grace, I would have thought it should be obvious. I wish to have my charges settled—permanently. What better way, I ask you, than to have you pick one of them for your wife?"

Willie and Andy tried to make a break for it, but were halted in mid-flight when Harry's hands clamped down hard on their respective shoulders. "My *what*?" he all but yelled. "Madam, you must be insane!"

Miss Stourbridge turned smartly on her heel and headed for the door. "I hardly think so, your grace," she said, not turning around. "After all, you must consider the alternative. You can't murder four women without raising some suspicion, and you can't just set us off to tell our sordid tale of revenge and rapine to anyone who will listen. I can think of at least three newspapers where my story would most likely gain an interested audience."

She stopped and turned to incline her head in farewell. "And now I must bid you good day, your grace, for it has been, all in all, a most exhausting day. I've already informed your butler—Pinch, I believe the man said he was called—that the Misses Somerville and I will be taking our evening meal in the comfort of our rooms, so you may feel free to tear off strips of the lads' hides anytime from now until tomorrow without fear of upsetting any female sensibilities."

4

TRIXY STOURBRIDGE retraced her steps to the west wing, her head held high, her footfalls even and purposeful, her outward appearance—although her gown was most depressingly outdated, a problem shared by her twin charges, who had dissolved into tears more than once while discussing the subject—one of complete and utter composure.

Inside, however, Trixy Stourbridge was a seething mass of apprehension.

His grace was so imposing, so fiercely masculine—so unexpectedly handsome. She was surprised she hadn't melted into a senseless puddle the moment she clapped eyes on him. Having prided herself on her ability to outwit any man, she had been momentarily taken aback by the cool shrewdness that had shown through the anger in Glynde's dark eyes.

Trixy had nearly forgotten what it was like to see some hint of intelligence peeping at her from the eyes of a man. She hadn't been gifted with that sight since the death of her beloved schoolteacher father six years earlier, an untimely death that had left Trixy all alone to face the world, and completely penniless into the bargain.

It had been a long six years, made even longer by the drudgery of the various employments she had been forced, without connections, without references, to accept in the interim. Her first positions had been more menial than instructive, and she had wiped far more childish noses than she had opened young minds to the glory of learning.

Difficult as it was to believe now, her position as governess-cum-companion to the Misses Somerville for the past two years had seemed to be a giant leap upward in her checkered career, with hopes of helping Myles Somerville present his beautiful blond twins to society in just a few short months acting as a carrot to give her lagging spirit the energy to go on.

That idyllic dream, the one that had a lot to do with Trixy hovering on the edge of some candlelit ballroom just as a rich, handsome peer of the realm strolled into the room, spied her, and immediately fell to his knees at her satin slippers, prostrate with adoration, had disappeared in a puff of smoke as she came to know Myles Somerville for what he was—and for what he wasn't.

He was, in a word, a crook. He wasn't, in a few more words, a very loving father. As a matter of fact, he couldn't even trouble himself to learn to tell Eugenie and Helena apart, an achievement that, thanks to their extreme likeness to one another, was not to be sniffed at, yet one a person would think a loving parent could master.

Within a week of their remove from Dorset to the metropolis, Trixy had all but decided that Myles planned to use his daughters, whom he had not visited above once or twice a year until they reached the age of eighteen, in order to line his own pockets —a not unusual ploy of fathers, but one that she could not find commendable.

Why, the man hadn't even possessed the intelligence to realize that his daughters could bring a fair price in the Marriage Mart of society. Had he never heard of the beautiful Gunning sisters and their amazing triumphs—never mind that one of them had eventually suffered an untimely end as a result of sipping arsenic to maintain her beautiful pale complexion?

Oh, no. He had harbored no plan to present Eugenie and Helena, had made no effort to replenish their badly depleted wardrobes or introduce them to eligible young gentlemen—a fact that quickly put paid to Trixy's own dreams of having herself discovered by a rich, handsome peer. Heavens, no. Myles Somerville hadn't planned on expending any of his blunt on anything as risky, as hit-or-miss, as the Marriage Mart.

Myles Somerville, Trixy had discovered only a week ago by the simple if not entirely praiseworthy process of applying one keen ear to a crack in the door between the hall and the sitting room while Somerville carried on negotiations with a particularly oily-looking gentleman, had come to London fully intending to sell his daughters to the highest cash bidder, without a word about marriage entering the conversation!

The duke's arrival in town had effectively spiked Somerville's guns—an unlooked-for circumstance that Trixy had viewed at the time as a gift from above—and Somerville had ignominiously stripped the town house of every portable asset, whether his or rented, and absconded, leaving his penniless girls to fend for themselves.

That last part, the bit about leaving his girls penniless, had tempered Trixy's elation at waving Somerville on his way out of their lives, so that she had ended by considering the Duke of Glynde's unknowing intervention as a mixed blessing.

Without funds, without prospects—without talent or great intellect—and with only their stunning beauty to aid them, it had appeared as if Eugenie and Helena would still end up being sold to the highest bidder, the only difference being that, with Myles Somerville effectively out of the way, they had eliminated the middleman.

Even worse, with Somerville gone, and with no one else to fend for them, it appeared as if it would be left to Beatrice Stourbridge to become that middleman—a terribly depressing thought.

Trixy's green eyes narrowed as she remembered something else she disliked about Myles Somerville. He had left his daughters behind, defenseless, to face the Duke of Glynde's revenge. She would have pointed that particular cowardice out to the man himself, only she couldn't be sure that he might not then have taken his girls with him—most probably to sell them to an oily Irishman rather than an oily Englishman.

As it was, she had, quite unwillingly, become the

chief defender of the girls' safety and honor, a daunting project given the fact that she had never been to London before, knew no one, and had no idea how to go on.

Trixy's face lost its pinched look as she recalled the events of the previous night, a comedy of errors that she had first become aware of as she had stumbled over Lacy's trussed-up body in the dark parlor on her way back from the kitchen, where she had been dozing over the table, her worries for the girls taking a momentary break as she had succumbed to a well-deserved nap.

Lacy had yet to fully forgive her for not unstuffing her handkerchief-muted mouth, but Trixy had known she would be courting disaster if the maid were free to scream, and had simply left the woman on the floor while she crept to her own room and unearthed her father's pistol. After that, it had been a simple matter to train that same pistol at the intruders—inept boys that they were—while a plan tumbled willy-nilly into her head.

And so far, she congratulated herself as she turned into the west wing of the truly magnificent Glynde country home, that plan had been ticking along quite nicely, with all the little pieces beginning to drop into place.

It had been no great gamble to rely on the duke's sense of honor, for any man who sought to revenge himself on the reprehensible Myles Somerville had certainly earned her vote! She harbored no real fears that the duke would set the girls and herself out on the road, any more than she could bring herself to believe the man would do them bodily harm in order to protect his rascally young brother.

Not, she reasoned, unerringly heading for the bedchamber where Eugenie and Helena lay napping, that she truly expected the duke to marry either of the girls—especially now that she had met him. If the poor man were ever to do murder, marriage to either one of the girls should be just the thing to push him to it. She had only put forth the idea in order to keep William and Andrew in line, having astutely judged the boys as dyed-in-the-wool romantics.

All she really wanted for the girls was some sort of income, and perhaps a small Season in London— surely nothing beyond the power of the overwhelmingly wealthy Duke of Glynde to arrange. That, and the allowance she had demanded for herself.

Her chin tilted upward as she reaffirmed her resolve to get herself out of this pickle with enough money to put a firm period to her days as paid companion—and if it was scraping very close to blackmail, well, what of it? She refused to allow her conscience to prick her on the subject.

Opening the door to the large, beautifully decorated bedchamber that housed her charges, she stepped inside to see Lacy still busily engaged in unpacking the girls' worn but perfectly matched belongings—the same ones Lacy had painstakingly packed into trunks while Trixy had held the boys at gunpoint.

"And were ye seein' his worship, missy?" Lacy asked, turning to look at Trixy. "He was as mad as a Methodist at an Irish wake, I'll be thinkin', to hear wot his featherbrained brother and his Friday-faced ruffian friend done."

Trixy collapsed gratefully into a nearby chair, kicking off her slippers and then wiggling her bare toes in ecstasy. "His grace took it all rather well, Lacy—although for a moment there I thought he was going to choke the life out of poor young Lord William," she told the maid, resting her weary head against the back of the chair. She laughed shortly in reminiscence. "As a matter of fact, I think the man was relieved to hear some sort of bad news from the boy, since he seemed to expect some. And to think, Lacy, that I've believed it difficult to ride herd on young girls. At least they don't abduct young boys, do they?"

"And his worship agreed ter yer plans?" Lacy asked, stuffing the last set of matching gowns into the wardrobe. "He's goin' ter wed my darlin' little Eugenie?"

Trixy rolled her eyes. "He hasn't even met your darling little Eugenie, Lacy. Give the poor man time to get used to the idea that he has two eligible unattached females under his roof before you ask him to make a choice between them."

"And will I be gettin' to stay with m'darlin'?" Lacy might not have been the brightest woman on earth, but she was well aware that the fate of one single Irish lady's maid would not be weighing heavily over his grace's head at the moment, what with him dealing with Trixy Stourbridge's demands.

Trixy laughed out loud as she looked across the room to the large bed where two sleeping blond heads could be seen peeping above the coverlet, two most angelic faces, beautiful in repose. "The duke may be a powerful man, but I don't think even he is strong enough to separate Eugenie from you, Lacy. I know I should never even attempt such a cruel division. For one thing, Eugenie's resultant vocal protests would most probably lift the roof right off this great house." She rose, stooping to pick up her shoes. "Now, if you don't mind, I think I'll go to my own room to unpack before dinner is served. We'll eat in here, I believe."

The maid nodded, turning back to the trunks, where she nearly upended her short, round body as she dug in the bottom of the larger one to retrieve the Misses Somerville's jean half-boots, her fears now settled so that she felt no qualms at not offering to help Trixy—who was, after all, naught but a slightly higher-placed servant—with her unpacking. "I'll give ye a holler when the vittles get here."

Trixy rubbed at her stiff neck. "You do that, Lacy," she said, shaking her head as she fairly dragged herself out of the room. What had she expected? she asked herself—a hug, a pat on the head, a simple "thank you, miss"? In the two years she had known Lacy and the girls, she had acted the protector, the budget stretcher, the—for lack of a better word—parent. Nobody thought to thank her—they just assumed she would take care of everything. Parenthood, she decided firmly, was a thankless job.

As she stood in the center of the small chamber she had allocated for herself, Trixy sighed, realizing that she was being poor-spirited. She didn't need any thanks, and most probably would have been embarrassed to hear them. She wanted only what was fair. She wanted her independence.

Smiling as she remembered the stunned look on the Duke of Glynde's face as she had told him the conditions for her silence, Trixy refused to acknowledge the niggling doubt deep in her breast that what she was doing was absolutely fair.

5

HARRY STARED into the bottom of his wineglass, trying to figure out just when it was that he had lost control of his life. Could he trace it back to the moment he had first heard the name Myles Somerville and learned that the man had bilked his late father out of some thirty thousand pounds? Or had it been that certain hour two weeks previously, when he had learned that this same Myles Somerville had taken up residence in London, and had decided to go after the man, with murder on his mind?

Could that have been the decisive moment—the turning point—the terrible, anticipated transgression that had, through its own selfish motive of revenge, stripped him of his control over his destiny?

Was he only experiencing the retribution of some higher authority who had decreed that Harry Townsend, sinner, should learn to repent for his evil thoughts having to do with taking dead aim at Myles Somerville's chest and then blowing a clean hole right through it?

Glynde sniffed audibly, then downed the remainder of his wine. He doubted it. He doubted it highly. No, to be absolutely precise about the thing, the reins of destiny had been wrenched from his hands long ago—the moment his parents had decided to further ensure the Glynde line into the next generation by means of the production of a second son.

William. His brother.

How Harry loved him.

How Harry longed to submerge the boy in boiling oil.

How could Willie have done this to him?

Pinch entered the study quietly and refilled his employer's glass before, as he watched the duke out of the corner of one eye, he laid another log on the fire and tiptoed back out of the room.

Harry belatedly grunted his thanks to the man and picked up the glass, holding it against the firelight to watch as the burgundy seemed to burn from a small fire within itself. He'd be good and drunk soon, if he could just keep drinking. Drunk enough to forget William's earlier explanations that had seemed to have a lot to do with blaming Andrew Carlisle for all their troubles and very little to do with laying any of the credit for this latest debacle at his own door.

Andrew, that born-to-be-hanged scoundrel, had manfully taken on the blame once all had been explained, an occurrence that hadn't surprised Harry, as he knew that the boys would do anything to help each other, and since it was not Harry's place to punish Andrew—which, considering Glynde's mood, was a very good thing for Andrew—his confession did nothing more than blunt the sharp edge of the duke's anger.

Glynde took a long sip of wine. What did it matter, anyway? The deed was done, the women were upstairs, and the scandal had to be suppressed. He put down the glass, his heart heavy. He couldn't drown himself in drink; he had to think. Somehow, in some way, he had to come up with a reasonable explanation that would divert his Aunt Amelia from the truth and at the same time enlist her aid.

The woman had, thankfully, remained in London for an extra day—the delay having something to do with modistes or milliners, or some such feminine foolishness—and it would be up to Harry to explain away the Misses Somerville once Aunt Amelia returned to Glyndevaron. His dark eyes hardened as he glared into the flames. And that Stourbridge chit had better go along with whatever story he made up or he'd see her carted away to jail for her pains—and the devil take the hindmost!

"Hullo. Goodness, it is dark in here, isn't it? Are you drinking alone? Trixy says a man who drinks alone is a man who drinks because he has to, not because he wants to. Is that true? Are you a sot? Trixy says England is thick with sots, that you can't go more than three feet in London without running into one of them. They'd drink ink if there was nothing else handy, so needful are they of liquid solace. I think Trixy doesn't like to see people drink. What do you think, your grace? You are the duke, aren't you? I mean, you don't much resemble Willie, but I should think no one but the duke could sit in here and drink wine all alone without somebody putting up a fuss. Isn't he simply adorable? Willie, that is."

Harry leapt to his feet, nearly tipping over the small table holding the wine decanter as he all but gaped openmouthed at the apparition standing just inside the doorway.

It was an angel—no, that would mean he really was drunk. It was a young girl, the most beautiful scrap of femininity he had ever been privileged to lay eyes on, drunk or sober. She was small; she was petitely, perfectly formed. She was golden from head to foot—from the hem of her sunshine-yellow nightrobe to her waist-length spun-gold curls. Her eyes were huge, and sky blue—opened wide in innocence and framed by ridiculously long black lashes. Her lips were a marvel—soft, full, and naturally pink—at least three shades deeper than the natural, healthy flush on her flawless cheeks.

As a matter of fact, if the apparition had not spoken, advertising her extreme youth, Harry would have said she was perfect.

"Who . . . who are you?" he managed to articulate, still staring, mouth remaining agape.

The "apparition" put a hand to her mouth and giggled. "I shouldn't be here, should I? I should be upstairs, tucked up in my bed—but I'm much too excited to sleep." She advanced into the room. "I'm Helena, by the way, Helena Adriana Theresa Somerville. Trixy says I'm not ever to embroider all my various initials on anything, or else people should think I'm selling hats. Do you understand? Helena—

H, Adriana—A, Theresa—T, and Somerville . . . well, you must have figured it out for yourself by now. Isn't Trixy funny? Did you really plan to murder my papa? I shouldn't wonder, as he is an odious man. Trixy says so."

Harry blinked twice, trying to reconcile Helena's inane chatter with the vision of ethereal beauty she presented. He was supposed to wed this creature? Live with this girl? Listen to this girl? The bloody hell he was! Only if he were to be struck deaf on his wedding night!

But wait, there were two of them—wasn't that what Willie had said? Surely they couldn't both be so empty-headed, could they? He closed his eyes and lifted a silent prayer that the twins were identical in everything but intelligence.

He motioned for Helena to take the seat he had so abruptly vacated, then excused himself to walk to the hallway to fetch Pinch. It was one thing to have Myles Somerville's daughters in his house temporarily by way of blackmail; it was entirely another kettle of fish to have himself compromised into the bargain. He wasn't sure how Pinch would feel, being employed as chaperon, but with Aunt Amelia absent, neither he nor the butler had much choice in the matter.

Pinch, however, was nowhere to be found. Instead, once he had passed into the hallway, the duke came face-to-face with Miss Beatrice Stourbridge, clearly a woman with a mission.

"Where do you have her?" she demanded, looking about the hallway as if Glynde had somehow stuffed the Somerville chit under a nearby table. Beatrice's long single braid whipped from side to side as she completed her visual inventory of the hallway and whirled about to face him. "I was just counting noses upstairs and found that Helena has gone missing. You have seen her, haven't you? She wouldn't have been so silly as to go searching after Willie again."

"Again, Miss Stourbridge . . . Beatrice?" the duke questioned, one eyebrow rising in confusion. "She went 'William hunting' earlier tonight? Whatever for?"

"Call me Trixy, if you please," she commanded shortly, brushing past Harry to enter the study. "I can't abide 'Beatrice,' and 'Miss Stourbridge' is entirely too formal for two people who are dealing on the level upon which we two are being forced to operate. Helena? Are you in here? Come out, come out, wherever you are—you headstrong little minx."

The duke sidled up behind her. "And I imagine you may address me as Harry—although for the life of me I don't know why I just said that. Stop fluttering about like an ancient hen who has misplaced her one chick. She's over there—good Lord, she's asleep in my chair! How could she do that?"

Trixy turned to look at him, a smile teasing the corners of her mouth. "Ancient hen? I'm at my last prayers, I agree, but I hadn't thought I was ancient. I think, Harry, that I must take umbrage at that statement."

Harry bowed from the waist, returning her smile. "My profound apologies, Trixy. It must have been the nightrobe that put me off. It is horrible, you

know. I have never been fond of plaid. Now, back
to the matter at hand—how do you suppose Helena
could fall asleep so fast?"

"It's the quick, untroubled sleep of the innocent
—which is another way of saying the little darling
doesn't have the intelligence to work up to a bout
of insomnia. Help me get her to bed, will you?"

Harry put a hand on Trixy's arm to stop her.
"Just a moment, Miss Stour . . . Trixy. What did she
want with my brother?"

Shaking off his hand, Trixy crossed the room—
the duke hard on her heels—to stand, hands on hips,
staring down at Helena. "It's quite simple, really.
She thinks your brother—the young miscreant who
planned to kidnap her and then set her up to be
ravished—is adorable. What can I say, Harry? The
child isn't overly bright."

His grace looked down wistfully on the angelic
face. "And her sister?" he asked, voicing his earlier
thoughts aloud.

"Eugenie? Why do you ask? Oh, don't tell me—
you're already trying to decide which of the twins
is to become your duchess. I must say, Harry,
you're not too slow off the mark, are you?"

Harry spoke through gritted teeth. "Just answer
the question, Miss Stourbridge."

"Trixy," she corrected, leaning down to give
Helena's shoulder a small shake. "And Eugenie is
much the brighter of the two. Not that that's saying
much," she added under her breath as Helena
opened her eyes, blinking in confusion.

"Oh, hullo, Trixy," Helena trilled, uncurling her
legs in preparation for rising. "Have you met the

duke? Yes, of course you have. You told us all about it at dinner. You were right. He is extremely handsome, in a dark sort of way—and he's quite old too. Not at all like Willie."

"Yes, pet," Trixy agreed tightly, longing to strike the child. Wasn't it bad enough that she had been forced to chase all over the house for the brat, finally running her to ground, only to present a view of herself to his grace while dressed in her shabby, frayed nightclothes? Did the child have to deal out glimpses of her earlier private statements about the man—and then insult that same man, into the bargain—although, of course, it did give him some of his own back for that nasty crack about ancient hens. Still, she couldn't help defending him. "I agree with you, darling, he's not at all like Lord William. His grace has all his second teeth. Now, come on, Helena. It's hours past your bedtime."

Harry leaned down to whisper once more in Trixy's ear, the feel of his warm breath tickling her throat and sending small shivers down her spine. "It would appear the two of us have one foot dangling into the grave, if this child is to be believed. Have you ever considered leading strings, Miss Stourbridge?"

"That—as well as a muzzle, your grace, although Helena doesn't think I'm old, just not very young," she answered quickly, leading her charge away. "And, please, the name is Trixy," she added as she paused at the doorway.

Harry lowered himself heavily into his chair, picking up his wineglass. "I shall try, madam, but I must tell you, I once had a pet rabbit named Trixy.

It seems odd to call a woman what I once called a pretty piece of vermin." He smiled, lifting the glass to her. He didn't know why, but he was feeling much more the thing than he had a few minutes ago. "Then again, as I think on it . . ." he ventured silkily, laughing as the governess fairly pushed Helena into the hallway.

Trixy took two steps back into the room. "How disappointing—and just when I had begun to believe I had finally met an intelligent man. You know, my father once had a large ugly green parrot named Harry," Trixy was stung into lying quickly, glaring at him so as to belie the fib. "He did a fearsome amount of talking, but he never had anything to say! And now, good night to you . . . Harry. Perhaps you should retire as well, for tomorrow you shall meet Eugenie and begin deciding which of your enemy's daughters you shall wed!"

Harry, alone once more, took a deep drink from his wineglass as he realized that Miss Trixy Stourbridge had a most disconcerting way of always getting in the last word.

6

"GOOD OLD HARRY," Willie murmured content-
edly, sighing in obvious delight as he lowered his
frame sideways into the overstuffed chair in the
sunlit morning room. "He's taking all this rather
well, isn't he? I mean, he has been a real brick about
everything, don't you think?"

Andy, already lying full-length on the settee, his
booted feet resting square in the middle of one over-
blown tapestry rose, tipped his head to the side and
contemplated the grin on his friend's face. "Do I
really think so, Willie? No, you gullible twit, I do
not, and neither would you if you stopped
congratulating yourself on your lucky escape long
enough to reason it out. I mean, consider the thing
carefully. Would you be happy to learn that Harry
had brought home two girls for you to marry?"

'Two girls for him to marry?" Willie shook his
head in disgust. Sometimes he wondered about
Andy. The fellow was his best friend, but there were
times he could be very silly. "Don't be such a Nick
Ninny. I never did any such thing. He can't marry

the both of them—that's not even legal, I don't think. Besides, I had no intention of bringing them here for Harry to marry."

"No, you wanted to bring them here to be ravished. Now that I consider it, I suppose Good Old Harry would have been over the moon about that."

Willie laid his head back over the arm of the chair, to stare up at the stuccoed ceiling and the dimpled *amorini* that cavorted there among flowing stucco ribbons and stars. "It all sounded so simple at the outset, didn't it? Now, here we are, knee-deep in women, and Harry is going about the house whistling, of all things. Maybe you're right, Andy. Maybe he isn't happy. Maybe he has just gone round the bend."

He sat up, turned about sharply so that his feet slammed against the floor, and looked at Andy searchingly. "Do you suppose that's it? Do you suppose m'brother's mind has snapped under the strain? My God, it must be—and it's all our fault!"

Andy was immediately caught up in the notion of the duke's tragic proposed addled mental state. Sitting up himself, he all but licked his lips, prophesying, "You shall have to lock him away, you know. Someplace like Bedlam—only cleaner. My cousin Bertram just came out from one of those private places, and he's fine as ninepence now—except for when there's a full moon, of course, but that's just a piddlin' thing compared to the way Bertram used to be. Wore a leather collar, for criminey's sake, and plopped onto the floor every time he had an itch, to scratch behind his ears with his foot. But he's out now, like I said, and received nearly everywhere—besides being heir to an earldom into the bargain. It can be done, Willie, if you just have faith."

Willie ran one hand distractedly through his blond locks. "Harry ain't crazy, you lump. He's too smart to be crazy. Don't talk stupid."

Andy spread his hands in disgust. "Me? Talk stupid? Hey, you're the one what brought it up in the first place. Wasn't me that started spouting off about any brother of mine going around spinning windmills in his head. Remember that, Willie."

"You don't have a brother, Andy," Willie pointed out reasonably. "You're an only child, with no hope of siblings. Your father says it's the single reason he can still face the dawn each morning. I've heard him say so a hundred times—maybe a thousand times."

Andy toppled back onto the couch, clutching his chest, his feet jabbing high into the air. "Oh, foul, foul! You've wounded me to the quick. Poor Papa! Poor Mama! Poor little Andy!" He sat up, stone-faced, to glower at Willie. "I am the veriest beast, a viper at the bosom, a heartless, thankless child. I ought to be horsewhipped."

"Oh, shut up," Willie said without rancor, gnawing at the side of his right thumb. "I have to think. It's just not normal. Harry isn't shouting. Harry isn't screaming. Harry, Lord help us, is whistling." He looked at his friend. "Why is Harry going about the place whistling, hmmm? Answer me that if you can, viper."

One answer popped so readily into Andy's head

that he couldn't believe Willie had not thought of it. "He rose earlier than we did this morning and has already seen the beautiful sisters Somerville? They *are* lovely little darlings, you know, Willie, even if I ain't much in the petticoat line m'self. And he gets to choose the one he likes best. Whistling? I'm surprised Good Old Harry ain't dancing a jig."

Willie frowned, shaking his head. "That's too easy, Andy," he pointed out, talkng even as he continued to worry at his thumb. "You have to remember the Stourbridge woman and her threats. Harry can't be taking that situation very lightly."

Andy nodded his agreement, for Willie's words rang true. Harry wasn't the sort to take kindly to blackmail. There had to be another reason for the whistle they had heard as the duke walked by them in the hallway. "Maybe he's planning to murder her," he said at last, unable to think of anything less bloodthirsty.

"Murder her!" Willie exclaimed, nearly jamming his thumb down his throat as he leapt to his feet. "My God, Andy, we've got to stop him!" He turned to run toward the doorway.

"Or maybe he isn't," Andy added quietly, causing Willie to stop in his tracks and sigh in relief. "Maybe he only intends to ship her off somewhere in the dead of night. Out of the way, without being put out of the way, if you know what I mean."

Willie nodded. "Yes—yes, that would work. He could drug her wine at dinner, truss her up while she sleeps, and have her placed aboard a ship heading to India—or maybe America. I know I wouldn't mind seeing her gone. I think she would have used that pistol, given half a chance."

Andy began pacing the floor, the bit between his teeth now. "Yes, and with Miss Stourbridge out of the way, the field would be clear to do what he willed with Eugenie and Helena in order to revenge himself on their father."

He turned to grin at his friend. "Why, you know what, Willie—we're right back where we started. You get to save your brother, I get to stay here until my parents return, and Harry gets to ravish a maiden—or both maidens, depending on his pleasure." He spread his arms wide. "All in all, Willie, I'd say my plan is working out very well. Very well, indeed!"

Willie took immediate exception to Andrew's last statement. "Your plan? *Your* plan! Now that everything's all solved, you're back—ready to take the credit. Isn't that just like you! And why wasn't it your plan when we were first trying to explain it to Harry? Answer me that, Mr. Brilliance!"

"I'd answer you that, Mr. Dullard!" Andy retorted hotly, pushing up his sleeves in preparation for doing battle. "It's my plan because you never had a single idea in your whole life worth so much as twopence. That's why it's my plan!"

"Oh, is that right?"

"Yes—that's right!"

Just when it appeared that the two friends were about to come to fisticuffs in the middle of the morning-room carpet, another, saner voice entered the conversation. "I thought so. I could hear the two of you bellowing out in the hall. Go ahead, boys, feel free to pummel each other into jellies. But I warn you, I've already sent a footman for a large bucket of cold water."

The cold water had only been mentioned, but its metaphorical application was enough to effectively douse the sparks rising from the boys' latest confrontation and, as usual, unite them as one against their common enemy, authority.

"We weren't fighting, Harry," Willie explained hastily, relaxing his fingers from the fists they had been clutched into moments earlier. "Fighting? Whatever would give you that idea? It was no such thing. We were just showing each other how Gentleman Jackson used to defend himself in the ring. We heard all about it in London, in a coffeehouse at the bottom of Bond Street. Didn't we, Andy?"

Andy nodded vigorously. "Cross-and-jostle work, the fella we met called it, isn't that right, Willie, my good friend? Yes, that was it—prime cross-and-jostle work." He turned to look unblinkingly into the duke's eyes. "It was ever so interesting, your grace—ever so interesting."

Harry just shook his head. "I don't know why lightning hasn't struck you down years ago, you miserable scapegrace—and you too, William—for the whopping lies you tell."

He held out a hand to stop his brother, whose mouth had opened, from saying anything further. "I don't want to hear it, William. Trust me in this, for I am not speaking idly. What I do want is for you both to sit down and listen to me for a change.

I've already requested that Miss Stourbridge and her charges remain in the west wing resting until tomorrow—keeping them out of the way. That leaves us this evening to deal with Aunt Amelia, who should arrive at Glynedevaron in time for dinner."

Willie grimaced at the mention of the woman's name. "Oh, Lord! I had forgotten about dotty old Queen Amelia. Do you think she'll cut up stiff?"

Harry pulled a face. "Cut up stiff, William? Our dearest Aunt Amelia? Just because she has, thanks to her dearest nephew, William, become part of the back end of a kidnap plot and likely to be sent to rot in jail, her good name dragged through the mud, her freedom gone, her courtesy role as chatelaine of Glyndevaron snatched from her grasp? Or— happy thought!—we might be able to keep it all quiet after all, and she will merely be cast in the role of abbess to a duo of unwilling mistresses. No, I don't think Aunt Amelia will mind at all. I shouldn't trouble my head if I were you, William. Why, I imagine she'll succumb to an apoplexy long before I can tell her the half of it."

While Andy prudently took two steps backward, away from the duke, Willie collapsed into a nearby chair, buried his head in his hands, and moaned pathetically. "She won't cock up her toes, Harry. That would be too easy. Oh, I think I'm going to be sick. Just what we don't need—Aunt Amelia running about willy-nilly, crying 'Off with their heads!' "

"Yes, she might do that too." Harry smiled, knowing he had at last succeeded in capturing his brother's attention. "But don't worry, boys," he added bracingly. "I may have thought of a plan to get us all out of this mess."

Willie hopped up as if he had springs hiden in his Hessians, his confidence in Harry shining in his eyes just as if he hadn't a few moments earlier been contemplating the terrible thought that his beloved brother had somehow lost a few slates off his intellectual roof.

"I knew it! I knew it! The minute I heard you whistling, I knew it! See that, Andy—I told you Good Old Harry wouldn't let us down. He has a plan!" A moment later he sobered, and turned to look at his brother. "What is your plan, Harry? You aren't going to make either of us marry the twins, are you? Andy and I . . . well, we hadn't either of us planned on settling down anytime just yet. No, of course not. You wouldn't do that to me. Oh, Harry—I love you, brother mine, truly I do!"

Harry took up the chair his brother had just vacated, crossing his long legs at the ankle as he inspected the nails of one hand. "If you've quite run down, William, perhaps you'll let me get on with my explanation."

He waited, hiding a smile, as his brother took a deep breath and settled himself, sitting at attention beside Andy on the edge of the settee.

"Thank you, children. I would be comforted by your obedient expressions if only I had not witnessed much the same set to your countenances last summer—precisely three seconds prior to the moment you told me a passing Gypsy had sold you a failure-proof formula to turn goat's milk into gold. Now, here's the plan . . ."

7

TRIXY WAS SO ANGRY she could barely see straight. How dare he? How dare the man challenge her in this way? Didn't he know that he was opening himself up to ridicule? Didn't he care? Was he so bent on revenging himself on her that he would go to these lengths to spike her guns?

"Of course he knows, the blackguard!" she told herself, looking down at the handkerchief she had shredded in her perturbation, then tossing it onto the bed. "Why else do you think he did it? It was too demeaning to his manhood to have been bested by a mere woman. If anyone is going to make a fool of the Duke of Glynde, he is determined it be himself. When will I ever learn?"

What bothered Trixy most was that she had not seen it coming. She had answered the late-afternoon summons to the duke's study ready to argue her case, prepared to refute any exceptions Glynde might have thought up to challenge her plans for him. Her hands had been steady, her chin held high. She was, she had convinced herself after a near-sleepless night, ready for any further objections he might care to throw at her.

What she hadn't been prepared for had been his offer.

"I have decided, Miss Stourbridge—Trixy—that we shall all remove to my London mansion within two weeks, to prepare for the Season," Glynde had announced glibly just as she was taking her seat across the desk from him.

"Prepare for the Season? All of us? Me?" she had heard herself blurt, knowing she was allowing him to see that he had caught her off-balance.

Glynde had steepled his fingers in front of his face. "Exactly. My brother and his thatchgallows friend, Andrew Carlisle, have done you and the Misses Somerville a grave injustice, and I, as the head of the family, mean to set things right. It is the only honorable thing to do."

Trixy had been immediately convinced she could smell a rat. A Season for the girls had been her dream, but there was something wrong. She was sure of it. "Go on," she had urged quietly, peering at him intently as he hid his expression behind his hands. "But, please, Harry, don't hide behind your 'honor.' What would be in this for you?"

Glynde had smiled then—and Trixy had longed to reach across the desk and slap him. "You're too quick for me, Trixy," he had answered, relegating her, by way of using her Christian name, to the ranks of young Lord William and his friend Andy. "I will not play coy and tell you I have forgotten that the twins are the offspring of Myles Somerville, my sworn enemy. But think on it a moment, Trixy.

What better revenge could I have than to very publicly pop the girls off, with Somerville not standing to make a penny on their marriages? From what I have heard while in London, I should think I would have then successfully stripped the man of the last of his assets."

"But think of the talk, Harry," Trixy had been stung into pointing out, not wishing to be a part of the scheme. "You'll be a laughingstock, sponsoring Eugenie and Helena. It's no secret that you loathe their father. To the world, it would look as if he had bested yet another Duke of Glynde."

"Possibly," the duke had admitted, "but I will know differently, which is enough for me. I would much rather the world thought I was a dupe than to have them believe I had contrived the heinous kidnapping of two innocent young females."

"And me," she had felt forced to add.

Harry's left eyebrow, she remembered, had risen at her words. "I said young females, Trixy. The innocent I leave to your conscience, considering that it was you who thought up the notion of blackmailing me for your silence."

"That's not what I meant, and you know it."

"No, I suppose it wasn't," Glynde had said, rising to signal that the interview was over. "As for you, Trixy, I shall expect you to go on as you have, chaperoning the girls—along with my aunt, Lady Amelia Fauntleroy, of course, who shall act as my hostess. At the end of the Season . . . well, I imagine you should be able to find adequate employment somewhere in London before the wages I've paid you to care for the girls runs out—if you cannot succeed in snagging yourself some eager widower looking for a mother for his runny-nosed children while you are squiring the girls about. I will give you a wage, as I wouldn't wish to be considered totally heartless, but that is all I will give you."

"So, you don't plan to give me my cottage and allowance? You had better think twice, your grace. I could leave this house now and go straight to the nearest newspaper office, to tell the world what your reckless brother has done," she remembered pointing out, refusing to rise from her seat.

"And who would believe you, Trixy?" he had answered, holding open the door to the hallway. "My aunt will be in residence before nightfall, and my servants are exceedingly loyal. It would be my word against yours. And remember, I've already met Helena. The girl is in no danger of becoming known as a bluestocking. It shouldn't be any trouble to convince the twins where their best interests lie. No," he had ended, smiling as Trixy began to walk, head down, out of the room, "I should think you'll see it my way in the end."

He had then held out a hand to grasp her elbow, detaining her for a moment more. "I will provide for the girls, I will replenish all your wardrobes, I will give the girls their Season, I will allow you to stay with them, in order to ease your mind, until they are married off. I will do all of this for you and the daughters of my enemy. But I warn you now, Miss Stourbridge, if a single word of anything that has happened between the moment Lord William first broke into the house on Half Moon Street and this moment reaches my aunt's ears, the whole lot of you will find yourselves sleeping under the hedgerows, my support withdrawn. Have I made myself clear . . . Trixy?"

"What possible plausible reason are you going to give your aunt for having Eugenie and Helena here?" she had asked, refusing to raise her head for fear he would see in her eyes the nervousness she felt standing so close to him, feeling his strong hand against her elbow. "Surely I should know, if I'm to instruct the girls in what and what not to say."

"That's simple, Trixy. I am prepared to tell my aunt that you, the devoted companion, prudently brought the girls to my door yesterday to beg my help, as Somerville had run off, leaving you all penniless. My aunt is a good woman, but she is not the possessor of an outstanding wit. She will accept what I tell her. I am to be a hero, I think, a selfless gentleman who has taken pity on three destitute women, believing myself to be at least partially responsible for your plight, as I was the one who scared off Somerville in the first place. Yes, Trixy, I believe I rather like that, don't you?"

"I don't think you care very much either way what I believe . . . Harry."

The duke's hand had finally dropped away from her elbow. "On the contrary, Trixy. I care very much what you think. After all, only consider where your 'thinking' has got us already."

Trixy had turned, looked up at the duke, opened her mouth as if to speak, and then shaken her head, turning away.

"What?" Glynde had challenged, his every word a dagger thrust to her heart. "No last words? No magnificent, cutting exit line? Why, Trixy, you disappoint me. Surely it isn't this easy to have the last word against you?''

But it had been that easy, Trixy recalled now, throwing herself across the bed on her stomach, to lie with her chin in her hands as she stared out the window at the gathering twilight. And what bothered her most was that she hadn't seen it coming.

She had been silently preening all day, congratulating herself for her brilliant coup in besting the Duke of Glynde. Her plan, conceived in self-defense, had quickly become personal—a battle of wills between the self-assured, handsome duke and herself, a poor, hardworking woman of no power and little prospects.

It had been David against Goliath, and the victory, although short, had been very sweet. But it was over now—and she hadn't even suspected that there had been a flaw in her scheme.

He had taken her plan and twisted it around to his own advantage, and while she admired his ingenuity, she hated him for his arrogance. If only she had been born a man, if only she had wealth and position behind her, if only . . .

"If only he weren't so handsome," she ended, laying her cheek against the satin coverlet. "If only there were some way I could turn into a gorgeous young lady and dazzle him with my beauty, my wit, my generous dowry. Then I should be on an equal footing with Harry—and entice him into losing his heart to me, only so that I could crush it mercilessly beneath my dancing slipper, just as he has so successfully crushed my brief dream of independence."

Trixy lay across the bed for a long time, until Lacy came to tell her that the dinner tray had been delivered across the hall to the twins' chamber.

"Coming, dearest Lacy," Trixy said brightly, rising quickly from the bed. And then she crossed the hall to eat a good dinner, chattering happily to the twins about their good fortune and the wonderful Season they would all share in London, measuring her words carefully, until, in the end, the twins actually believed that their come-out had been the plan all along.

Trixy might have had to force some of her gaiety, but her good mood did not rely entirely on her hard-learned ability to hide her true feelings. For Trixy Stourbridge had used her time lying across the bed wisely—and once more, she had a plan.

8

"EXCUSE ME, MA'AM," Trixy said politely, standing in the doorway of the main saloon just before noon of the following day. "Could you possibly be Lady Amelia? No, of course not. Silly me, to ask such a question. Harry has hinted to me that his Aunt Fauntleroy is a much older woman, a contemporary of his father's. You couldn't possibly be she . . . but you must be. How I shall roast Harry for bamming me with tales of how his darling aunt might be too fatigued to take on the role of hostess for the Season. I'm Trixy Stourbridge, by the way," she said, advancing into the room to curtsy in front of the woman, "companion to the Misses Somerville, Harry's wards."

Amelia Fauntleroy, a woman who would never see the sunny side of fifty again, held out her hand to Trixy, then patted the spot next to her on the sofa, urging the newcomer to sit down. "We have heard of your advent, Miss Stourbridge," she said, employing the kingly "we" with an ease that indicated the woman was comfortable in its usage, "and although we are still very much at sixes and sevens, what with thinking of all the intricate preparation that goes into the successful launch of two young misses, we are eagerly anticipating the event."

Trixy bit down hard on the inside of her cheek, trying not to give way to mirth. The woman was going to be so easy it might not be sporting. Sneaking an assessing look at Lady Amelia out of the corners of her eyes, Trixy took in the woman's self-satisfied expression, plumpness of face and figure, her watery blue eyes, her obviously dyed black hair, the flowing draperies of her gown, and the four rings that all but cut off the circulation in four of her pudgy fingers. Oh, yes. This was going to be very easy.

"Then you are pleased!" Trixy trilled, clapping her hands delightedly. "Oh, dearest Harry was right—you must be the very best of aunts. Just wait until you meet Eugenie and Helena, Lady Amelia. You'll be immediately taken with them, as they are wonderful girls. So biddable, so freshly beautiful. Truly, ma'am, diamonds of the first water—and so very grateful to you and dearest Harry for all you are prepared to do for them."

Lady Amelia smiled at the flattery even as she frowned in confusion. "We do not quite understand this familiarity with my nephew," she admitted, picking at the lace on the skirt of her gown. "His grace has given you permission to address him as Harry? It's most odd, we think."

Trixy bent her head and held her breath until her cheeks became flushed, as she had never been able to blush on command, no matter that she was a fair-skinned redhead. She couldn't bring herself to lie to the woman, but that didn't mean she had to tell the complete truth, did it?

"Oh, dear me," she said with a nervous giggle, "I thought you knew, Lady Amelia. I'm so embarrassed. Harry has been so very gracious as to allow me to address him informally, as he, in turn, does me. He . . . he's a very sweet man, isn't he? Please tell me you don't mind. I wouldn't wish for you to be angry with Harry. He has been so kind—taking me in, offering to provide me with an entire new wardrobe so that I may take part in the Season as well. Oh, yes. He expressly said that he harbors the belief that I too, and not just the girls, might be satisfactorily settled before the Season is over." Find herself a widower, would she? Harry would rue the day he had jabbed her with that dart, she thought, fluttering her lashes demurely.

Lady Amelia giggled. Trixy could hardly believe what she was hearing, but it was a definite girlish giggle. "Oh, that Harry—what a card!" Lady Amelia trilled, laying one beringed hand on Trixy's forearm. "We think we are beginning to see the reason behind my nephew's uncharacteristic act of charity. He must have seen you when he went to Half Moon Street to call out that odious Myles Somerville and become instantly smitten. No wonder he took you in when you applied for his help. We couldn't believe he would willingly take on the debut of two young ladies, daughters of his enemy, but now we understand. He has another, eminently more personal reason for helping those poor girls, hasn't he? Were you taken with Harry on sight as well, dearest girl?"

Trixy placed her hand over the older woman's and patted it. "Truly, ma'am, I don't believe you have the right of it. Harry was just being kind. I doubt he cares a snap for me. As a matter of fact, I'm not even sure he likes me very much. It's the girls who concern him, who have touched his tender heart. You mustn't read romance into his simple act of charity."

Lady Amelia nodded sagely. "We understand your meaning completely, my dear, and we shan't tease him with our knowledge. We always knew it would take a more mature woman to pique his interest. We cannot wait to get you to London and outfit you in a way that will dazzle Harry. It shan't be easy—your hair presents quite a problem, you understand—but we shall consider that a challenge. Oh, but it will be fun to watch Harry try to elude the callings of his heart, my dear, truly it will. For so long we have feared that Harry would never wed, that he was taking this duke business too seriously, but now . . . well, just let us say that we are very pleased."

As Trixy allowed herself to be enveloped in a perfumed hug, she decided that dishonesty, once the first faltering step had been taken, rapidly became increasingly easy to repeat. She had a roof over her head for the Season, the promise of an entire new wardrobe, the wages Harry promised to pay her, and with only a little luck, she would end up with the cottage and allowance as well.

9

THE DUKE OF GLYNDE was perplexed. He wasn't exactly sure what he had been expecting the atmosphere of Glyndevaron to be once he'd made his announcement—complete with carefully calculated fibs—to his Aunt Amelia, but he was certain that he had not gotten what he had expected, for the general mood inside the house for the succeeding forty-eight hours had bordered on the euphoric.

His aunt, for one, couldn't be happier, nor more nearly incoherent in her joy. She was "absolutely taken" with Eugenie and Helena and all but promised her nephew that, together, the beauteous twins would take London society by storm.

And, according to his aunt, Trixy Stourbridge was "a rare treasure," a young woman so good of heart and unselfish of spirit that she did not make a single demand for herself, caring only for the good of the twins; her modest nature made it imperative that Aunt Amelia see to it that the companion be rigged out in all the latest fashions and be forced, if necessary, to join in all the fun of the Season.

The fact that each statement Aunt Amelia made about Trixy was punctuated with an "I know more than you think I know, you little dear" wink did nothing to ease the duke's mind.

Willie and Andy, obviously believing themselves to have personally contrived this happy resolution of their latest idiocy, had immediately washed their hands and consciences of the entire project, and were now returned to their previous all-absorbing pursuits—most of them having to do with causing as much trouble as possible, all in the name of fun.

Miss Trixy Stourbridge, the duke recalled, suppressing a shiver, appeared to have taken her defeat with a graciousness that stunned as well as worried him. She had kept almost completely out of sight these past four days, closeting herself with the twins and his aunt, making preparations for their removal to London.

It was only at dinner that Harry saw her, and then she was seated below the salt, so that he could not engage her in conversation without yelling down the table at her, a thing he wasn't about to do, and they hadn't exchanged more than polite greetings since their last uncomfortable meeting in his study.

Guiding his horse along the ice-rimmed path through the home wood, Harry mentally berated himself for looking for demons where none existed, but he knew he couldn't help himself. Everything was going well—too well. With any luck, he should be shed of the twins within the next few months, his good family name intact, while at the same time providing his aunt with a well-deserved diversion in the city.

Ridding himself of the twins could likewise remove Trixy Stourbridge from his world, an event to be anticipated with the same eagerness with which he would view ridding his fields of a plague of grasshoppers.

Glynde grumbled and pulled his wool muffler up over his mouth and nose to block the icy wind that was the only remnant of the late-winter storm that had struck the area two days previously. He did want Trixy out of his life as soon as possible, didn't he? What a silly question! Of course he did. She was a scheming, blackmailing, nasty-tongued troublemaker, and the sooner he was shed of her, the better!

Turning his horse toward the house, Harry sighed, knowing what was bothering him. He had to face it, confront this demon, and stare it down. There was no getting around it. Trixy—terrible, common name!—Stourbridge was a fascinating woman.

She had a mind, for one thing, which was a singular accomplishment for a female, or at least for females of his acquaintance. She also had an air of competence about her—she gave off a certain undefinable impression of common sense. And she was brave. A person had to be brave to take on two male intruders in her household. A person had to be even more brave to take on the Duke of Glynde in his own household.

Of course, a person might also dare those two things if that person were brick stupid or had no sense of self-preservation, but the duke did not believe that to be the case with Trixy. She had known just what she was about, even if she couldn't have foreseen how he—her superior in every way—would neatly checkmate her move.

She was a worthy adversary, and she took defeat well, without tears, recriminations, or threats of revenge. She took defeat, to be plain about the thing, like a man! Harry admired that.

He also admired her warm auburn hair that shone with golden lights when the candlelight caught it, her smooth pale skin, her deep emerald eyes, and her straight, trim figure. He hadn't seen many redheads, and the ones he had met were usually short, prone to chubbiness, and got spots all over them when they went out in the sun. Trixy's skin leaned more toward ivory, and was flawless.

"Her figure is flawless as well, and curves in all the right places," Harry muttered from behind his muffler, immediately cursing himself for his lascivious thoughts.

He had better get Trixy Stourbridge out of his head until he could get her out of his house. She was dangerous.

Glynde was about to turn his mount for home when he heard a female scream, followed by a high, childish giggle. The sound hung in the cold air for a moment, only to be fractured by the deeper, more full-throated sound of a man's hearty laughter. William's hearty laughter, to be exact.

With thoughts beating in his head of his ramshackle brother having thrown another spoke into the works by taking one of the Somerville twins out without a chaperone—so that Trixy would make sure he ended up with a wedding in the house anyway—Harry spurred his mount forward toward the pond, sure the sounds had emanated from that area.

The sight that met his eyes once he'd rounded the corner beyond the Grecian ruin his mother had ordered built twenty years previously was one of innocent fun and youthful frolic.

The storm had caused the large, nearly circular, carefully constructed pond to freeze over from shore to shore, and the four youngest residents of Glyndevaron were on the ice, the twins seated on old wooden chairs, the boys behind them on skates, pushing.

"Faster, Willie, faster!" one of the rosy-cheeked twins commanded, holding on to the sides of the chair for dear life, her booted feet in the air. "Oooh! I feel so giddy!"

"Helena, behave yourself," warned Eugenie as Andy executed a dangerous maneuver, turning Eugenie's chair in a full circle so that they could avoid Willie as he, the chair, and Helena whizzed by. "I think I can see your ankles."

Harry smiled benevolently, watching as Willie lost his bearings and toppled to the ice, landing smack on the seat of his pants and causing no end of mirth in the others. Having already made out the squat dark figure of the maid, Lacy, on the far bank, huddled—shivering yet vigilant—close beside a small fire, the duke could find no harm in the scene.

In fact, the whole image was appealing. The trees surrounding the pond were still heavy with snow, their branches drooping gracefully down over the shiny surface of the pond. Through the bare branches could be seen glimpses of a startlingly blue sky, with the mellow pink stone of Glyndevaron visible near the left of the duke's line of vision. A warming afternoon sun caught each ice particle and turned the scene into a true winter wonderland, complete with two young, beautiful girls dressed in matching midnight-blue velvet pelisses and two youthful swains, their curly brimmed beavers sitting slightly atilt the top of their heads.

Harry longed to join them, for he hadn't been up on his skates since the winter his father had died. He sighed, remembering how carefree he had been that last winter upon his return from the Peninsula. He had truly been Good Old Harry then, as full of frolic and the love of life as his brother and Andy were now.

Growing up had come late to Harry, but abruptly, and he knew he was a far cry now from the carefree young man that he had been. Why, Willie at his worst had never even attempted the things Harry had done without thought. There hadn't been a rig he hadn't run, a local farmer he hadn't angered, a village girl he hadn't kissed.

He lifted his hands on the reins, ready to trot back to the house and rummage through his rooms until he found his skates, when a person-sized blob of drab dark gray entered the scene from the right, gliding smoothly across the ice. His hands froze as he realized that it was Trixy Stourbridge, her bonnet missing, her flaming hair tumbling free down past her shoulders, her gloved hands swinging gracefully from side to side as she skated along confidently.

As he watched, she hiked up her skirts a fraction and did a little leap into the air, coming down lightly and turning a full circle before heading out across the pond once more.

Harry continued to watch until she was out of sight beyond the other side of the ruin, his teeth clenched so tightly his jaw was beginning to ache. She skated with such confidence, with such freedom—such abandon! She skated the way he had skated before the cares of the world had made him forget what it was like to push out strongly across the frozen pond, his muscles straining, his head thrown back into the wind, his heart pumping with the exhilaration of nearly flying, soaring like a bird on the wing.

A minute later and she was back, her smile wide, her eyes twinkling as if the sun had found tiny sparks inside them and set them dancing. She performed that lightfooted leap once more before skidding to a stop alongside Andrew.

"Trixy," the duke heard Eugenie trill, "you look truly wonderful on the ice. I shouldn't be so brave if I lived one hundred years. Poor Andy here is quite bored, I think, pushing this frail spirit of mine about on a safe wooden chair."

"Are you quite sure you won't want to borrow these skates?" Trixy answered, while Harry leaned forward on his mount in order to hear her every word. "They are a little big for me, and clumsy, but I'm sure that his grace wouldn't mind."

Harry began to see the white winter scene through a haze of angry red. It wouldn't do him any good to go back to the house for his skates. His skates were already here—and that insufferable Stourbridge woman had them strapped to her boots!

Was nothing sacred anymore? Wasn't it enough that he had committed himself to squiring Myles Somerville's offspring all over London? Wasn't it enough that he was feeding four extra women, clothing three of them, housing all of them, and preparing to shovel out the blunt to pop two of them off? Did he have to sacrifice his skates as well?

He by bloody damn Jupiter did not!

"Miss Stourbridge!" Harry called out loudly. Dismounting, he tied the reins to a nearby branch and walked toward the edge of the pond. "Come here a moment, if you please."

The smile she had been wearing, the smile that had lighted up her whole face and made him forget the drabness of her clothes and the method she had used to enter his life, faded as she skated toward him. "You bellowed, Harry?"

"You're wearing my skates," he said, hating the childish tone of his voice. Why, in a moment he'd be whining like some puling infant. "I . . . I wonder if you'd mind relinquishing them for a few minutes, while I take a turn on the ice myself."

Trixy bit at her bottom lip. "I don't know, Harry," she answered a moment later, looking at him assessingly. "As I was just about to tell the boys, I think the sun has begun to do its work farther out on the pond, where the water is deeper. That's why

I have decided that this turn was my last. With your weight, I believe—"

Pique made Harry testy—and proportionately foolhardy—so that he was not about to heed the advice of a mere female. He wasn't some giant elephant, to go crashing through what he could clearly see was a good solid stretch of fist-thick ice. She just didn't want to give up the skates—he was sure of it. She knew, deep inside, that he was the superior skater, and didn't want to be shown up in front of her charges and the boys. All this and more the duke thought.

But "I'll be careful" was all he said, his smile tight and fleeting as he helped her clomp in ungainly fashion through the snow on the shore of the pond to sit herself down on a fallen log.

It is truly amazing how a skill, once learned, comes back easily even after an absence of three years. Within five minutes Harry had rid himself of his riding cloak and was on the ice, joking with his brother as Willie dared him to perform the jump that had been his grace's own particular invention. Harry quickly agreed, and the girls were unceremoniously transferred to the bank so that the boys could position the two chairs back to back in the center of the pond.

"Five pounds says he falls on his rum . . . um . . ." Andy hesitated, looking down at Eugenie, who was frowning worriedly. "That is to say, five pounds says that he can't do it!" he ended, challenging Willie to take the bet.

"Oh, yeah? Ten pounds says he'll sail over the both of them with room to spare!" Willie answered immediately, as Helena took hold of his arm and looked at him adoringly, batting her long dark lashes and—yet again—giggling as if overwhelmingly amused. "Fifteen pounds!" Helena's giggles goaded William into shouting. "Twenty—and my bay mare for a week!"

"Harry," Trixy called from the shore, "please reconsider. Skating is one thing, but to actually jump on that ice? I really don't think—"

Glynde turned to bow in her direction, his smile now broad and fixed as if frozen in place. "Thank you, ma'am, for those kind words of encouragement. Don't concern yourself—I've been skating here since I was old enough to strap on my first skates. And I promise, I won't show you up—at least not too much."

With the girlish squeals of the twins, the rallying cheers of the boys, and Trixy's worried frown to speed him on his way, Harry pushed off, staying close to the shore as he worked to build up speed. Once, twice, he circled the outer reaches of the pond, his lungs burning with each gulp of frigid air, the muscles in his long, strong legs straining as he used them as they had not been used for more than three long years.

He lost his hat as he whizzed by the watching group on the third time around and never noticed that it was gone. His coattails flew out behind him like tail feathers and the tasseled ends of his muffler waved like plaid flags.

Heart pounding, exhilaration singing in his ears, he sought out his favorite launching spot—a small space near the narrow end of the pond where there were no trees and the wind came straight at his back—and made his last turn before attempting the jump.

There was nothing in front of him now but the two chairs, the top of their high backs a good four feet off the ice. He'd have to remain in the air for the space of at least six feet, he figured hastily, but he wasn't worried. Why, he had already jumped three chairs—and once, four chairs.

He couldn't hear the birds singing high above him in the trees.

He couldn't hear the cheers from the shore.

All Harry could hear was the rasping of his own breath behind the muffler and the sound of his metal runners scraping across the ice.

It was time to fly, time to float above the ice, his knees bent to his chest, his head and shoulders flung front, his arms wide for balance.

He could feel his muscles bunching to supply the burst of power he would need to launch himself into the air—and then he was going up, up, the chairs passing underneath him as he flew above them with nearly half a foot to spare.

Now there was no sound, no scrape of metal against ice, no rasping breath, since he had taken in a great gulp of cold air at the last moment and trapped it deep in his lungs.

Now there was only quiet.

And then he landed, one foot slightly in front of the other, his arms tilting this way and that like twin rudders, keeping him upright, and the sounds of the world came rushing back.

Harry heard his own grunted gasp as his body

absorbed the rude shock of the landing. He stopped four feet in front of the chairs, to take his well-deserved bow.

Harry heard the shouts and squeals from the shore as Willie danced about on one foot, calling, "Huzzah! Huzzah!"

Harry heard birds calling in the trees, his horse's whinny . . . and the faint crackling sound of splintering ice.

Splintering ice? Splintering ice! Glynde looked down at his feet to see an ever-widening spiderweb of cracks flowing out in every direction. The sound grew louder, and he whirled around to see that a hole had opened behind him and one of the chairs was already bobbing on top of the water.

He looked toward the shore to see that Eugenie or Helena—he couldn't be sure which, and didn't much care at that moment—had gracefully swooned into Andy's arms.

Trixy was yelling to him, telling him to get down and crawl toward them slowly, a notion Harry didn't favor, as he didn't relish the thought of what he would look like scampering about on all fours like a hound. Instead, he gingerly placed one foot in front of the other, his gaze steady on the bank that suddenly seemed to be a mile away.

Within the space of a heartbeat Harry was skating uphill on ice that was tipping into the ever-widening hole behind him. Slowly, so that it almost seemed like something out of a bad dream, he felt himself descending, still upright, into the pond.

As the water closed over his head, the last thing

"Good Old Harry" did was curse that miserable Beatrice Stourbridge for wishing this disaster on him.

10

"THERE YOU GO, HARRY—now, open your mouth like a good little soldier. Oh, come on, Harry. It's only a bit of broth. I don't see why you're making such a fuss about it."

The Duke of Glynde eyed the spoonful of steaming liquid wearily. "Who made it?" he asked, holding the covers protectively in front of his mouth.

Lord William, perched on the side of the high, wide bed, replaced the spoon into the bowl. "Well, I don't see what that has to do with anything, but if you must know, I think Trixy—Miss Stourbridge—made it. Now, will you eat it?"

"I thought so. It doesn't smell like anything Angelo ever prepared for me." The covers moved up a fraction. "In that case, I most definitely don't want it. Not a drop."

"Oh, give over, Harry," Willie scolded, rising to set the bowl on a side table. "It has been three days; don't you think you could stop blaming Trixy for your accident? After all, she was the one who devised your rescue, you know."

"And I don't want to hear that miserable story again, William," the duke warned his brother testily, lowering the covers a fraction now that the bowl was safely out of the way, uncaring that he must appear fractious. "Anyone would suppose you're thinking of applying to Prinny himself, asking to have the miserable woman knighted."

Willie paid his brother no attention at all, immediately launching himself into a recitation of his latest hero's—heroine's—achievement. "There we were, all of us, standing on the bank completely helpless while you slowly sank into the pond, looking for all the world like a ship going down in a storm, when Trixy ordered us to tie all our coats and cloaks together to make a rope."

"I repeat, since you didn't seem to understand me: I don't want to hear it!"

"It was magnificent, really, how quickly she organized us, what with Eugenie fainting all over Andy the way she was," Willie persisted, gazing into the middle distance as if visually reliving the scene. "Tying the sleeves of the last coat tightly around my waist, Trixy had me crawl onto the ice on my belly, but I must have been too heavy, for the surface began to crack some more."

"William, if you bear me any affection, any affection at all—"

"That's when Trixy took it upon herself to go out onto the ice, risking life and limb to save you—you, who hasn't had a kind word for her, before or since." Waving his hands back and forth slowly above his head, as if to demonstrate Trixy's actions,

Willie continued, his voice hushed in awe, "She slithered like a snake—without a single thought of herself—until at last she grabbed hold of the collar of your jacket. You were bobbing up and down like a cork in a puddle, you know, so it was fairly easy to grab hold."

"Willie, I'm warning you—"

"We all heaved to on the chain of clothing—inch by terrible inch—until at last the two of you were back on shore." He turned to look down on his brother, frowning as he remembered what might have happened. "You could have drowned, you know, yet all you ended up with was a piddling dose of the sniffles. Trixy was magnificent, Harry. Truly magnificent."

Harry slunk down into the mattress, giving up the fight. Perhaps if he agreed with his brother for once, the lad might stop reciting the tale at the drop of a feather. "When you're right, you're right, Willie. Trixy was . . . magnificent."

Willie deposited himself heavily on the side of the bed once more. "Yes, yes she was—and now you won't so much as sip her broth. I have to tell you, Harry, I think it's mighty poor-spirited of you. We all of us do."

"You all do? Have you had a conference, then, Willie? Have you taken a vote? Tell me, am I to be horsewhipped the moment this damnable fever leaves me and I can get up from my bed? Or perhaps none of you will talk to me for a month. No, that can't be it. I'd never consider that a punishment— the resultant silence would be more in the way of a gift."

An impartial observer of this scene could not have

been faulted for believing that his grace, the Duke of Glynde, was behaving in a most surly, ungrateful, even self-pitying manner.

That impartial observer would, alas, have been correct.

The duke was behaving badly. The duke was feeling most exceedingly ungrateful toward his rescuer, as well as extremely put upon by his brother, who, along with every visitor he'd had since his dunking, had recited the facts of his rescue *ad nauseam*—Andy, in fact, had even employed props!

Yes, the duke, to be plain about the thing, would have liked nothing better than to forget the incident had ever happened.

But Harry's wish was impossible, for Glynde-varon was in the country, the countryside was gripped in the dragged-out end of a long, boring winter, and there was precious little to talk about other than the one piece of excitement to hit the estate since Willie and Andy had nearly set fire to the drawing room lighting the Yule log last Christmas.

The rousing tale of "The Dunked Duke" had permeated the household from attic to cellars, then traveled rapidly from stable to outlying farm. There was no avoiding it, there was no getting away from it, there was—as the long-suffering duke had learned to his complete disgust—absolutely no way to stop hearing it even in the privacy of his own bed-chamber, a place he had almost gratefully retired to at his first sneeze, on orders from the distressed Lady Amelia.

And it was all Trixy Stourbridge's fault! Harry had convinced himself of that the moment he'd heard the ice cracking beneath his skates, and nothing that had taken place since that moment had served to change his mind.

After all, if she had not been such a lax companion as to allow her charges to become part of an ice-skating party, none of this would have happened in the first place.

And if she had not pilfered his skates, and then all but dared him to try skating far out onto the pond—oh, yes, she had dared him, he was sure of it, for a warning was as good as a dare—he wouldn't have taken that leap . . . or broken through the ice . . . or had to be rescued . . . or be hiding out here in his bed, suffering from an annoying runny nose and this miserable fever—as well as the slings and arrows of outrageous fortune.

Did Harry, deep in his heart of hearts, know that he was being unreasonable? Yes. He knew it. Of course he knew it. He had fought it for the first two days, fought it mightily, but he was a reasonably intelligent man, and he realized that Trixy Stourbridge had not been the real cause of his dunking. Pride had pushed him out onto the ice; pride and a sinking feeling that he had taken on the trappings of adulthood at the loss of the freedom he had experienced as a youth.

But even though he was ready to admit his own culpability to himself, Harry was not ready to share that knowledge with anyone else. Above all, he was not ready to confront Trixy herself, for if he did, he would have to thank her for rescuing him—and that, to Harry, could only be seen as a fate even worse than that of an icy, watery grave.

"What are you thinking, Harry?" Willie asked at last, interrupting the duke's brown study. "Your forehead is all furrowed, as if you're lost in deep thought. Or are you in pain? Of course you are. How could I be so unfeeling as to tire you out this way? Should I send for the doctor again?"

"The doctor?" Trixy inquired concernedly from the doorway. "What's wrong, Willie? Can his grace have taken a turn for the worse? You should have rung for me at once."

"Rung for you, madam?" Harry bit out testily, turning his head to see that Trixy, not waiting upon ceremony, and most certainly not bothered by the notion that she, an unattached female, shouldn't be inside a grown man's bedchamber, was making her way purposefully to his bedside. "There's a pair of my breeches hanging over that chair in the corner. Perhaps you'd like to try them on for size?"

Willie screwed up his face, looking at Trixy. "Try on his breeches? Trixy, do you think Good Old Harry's gone delirious?"

Trixy shook her head, looking over to see the still-full bowl of rapidly cooling broth sitting on the side table. "He was never that sick in the first place. Good Old Harry, as you call him, Willie, is not delirious. Good Old Harry is simply being snotty." She leaned down to adjust his covers. "You *are* being snotty, aren't you, Harry?"

It took a great effort for Glynde not to snap back childishly, "I am not!" but he did it, limiting himself to a short snort of derision. "Are you comfortable, Trixy, running my household?" he asked, looking up at her.

"Quite comfortable, thank you," she answered, gently pushing Willie aside so that she could take his place on the bed. Reaching out a hand, she tested Glynde's forehead for traces of fever. "Oh, that's much better, isn't it, Harry? Your fever is all but gone, not that you ever had much of one in the first place. Now, if we could only get you to take some of this broth, we would all be happier."

"Which 'we' would that be, Trixy?" The duke asked wearily as he watched her retrieve the bowl and spoon from the side table. "I must warn you that you are beginning to sound distressingly like my Aunt Fauntleroy."

"I can think of worse fates," she responded easily, lifting the spoon toward his mouth. "Now, open up wide—oh, come on, Harry, it's nothing more than chicken broth."

"I don't want it," Harry said, tight-lipped. "I want some of Angelo's roast beef—rare, and with horse-radish sauce."

"I'm sure we all do, Harry, but that's impossible," Trixy answered placatingly, bringing the spoon closer. "Unfortunately, Angelo departed early this morning for London."

"What! Angelo has done what?" the duke bellowed just before the spoonful of broth was dumped onto his tongue. He swallowed the liquid down automatically. "Dammit, woman, what did you do to Angelo? William!" he called out, looking past Trixy to see that his brother was in the process of tiptoeing stealthily out of the room. "Don't move another muscle, William. Now, tell me, what has this miserable, managing woman done to Angelo?"

Willie, a hand to one ear, cocked his head toward the door. "Did you hear that, Harry? That was the dinner bell—I'm sure of it. And here I am, not even dressed for dinner. Harry, you know what a stickler Queen Amelia is whenever I try to come to table dressed in my dirt. Poor dear. I wouldn't want to upset her, would you? Well, I guess I'll have to be off. Trixy, you'll explain everything, won't you?"

The duke sat up, leaning on his elbows. "William, you traitor, come back in here this—uuummff!"

"There you go," Trixy said in obvious triumph, spooning another measure of broth into Harry's gaping mouth. "Now, isn't that good?"

The duke bit down on the spoon and pulled it free of Trixy's hand, the movement causing his dark hair to tumble down over his eyes. A moment later, the spoon still sticking from his mouth, the bowl of broth hit the far wall, having been hurled there by Harry himself. Two moments later, and the spoon had joined the bowl on the floor.

"There!" he declared forcefully. "Now, madam, unless you'd enjoy following where your broth has led, I most earnestly suggest that you tell me why my cook has been banished to London, a place, I might point out, in which I—his employer—am not currently in residence."

Trixy looked down pointedly at Glynde's hand, which was at that moment wrapped rather tightly around her forearm, then gazed into his face and smiled.

"Since you asked so nicely, your grace," she said

sweetly, "I should be happy to enlighten you. When last you went to London, Angelo was mightily dismayed by the state of your kitchens. The thought of enduring an entire Season working on your antiquated stove all but reduced the man to tears—Italians are so emotional, you understand."

"I don't believe this," Harry muttered under his breath, mourning the loss of his cook. "Go on—you might as well tell me the whole of it."

"Your aunt and I, fearful that the man might hand in his resignation—Lady Amelia having already told me of your great affection for Angelo's way with pastries—immediately suggested a renovation at the mansion. Angelo agreed, with the stipulation that he himself oversee the project." Trixy shrugged her shoulders. "Simple, isn't it, once it's explained? Will you release me now or is there something else I can help you with, Harry?"

Glynde's grip on her arm did not slacken, and when he spoke again, his voice was low and intense. "You've taken over, haven't you, Trixy? I don't know how you've done it—I'm not even sure *why* you've done it—but you have moved in, unwanted, and completely taken over my household."

Trixy returned his stare levelly. "Yes, Harry, I imagine you might believe that. But what else was I to do? Your aunt was all but hysterical after your accident, and the girls had to be considered. Surely you don't believe Lord William to be capable of running Glyndevaron?"

The duke's grip intensified. "Running Glyndevaron? What do you mean by that? I was speaking of my kitchens, my staff. My God, woman, I've been laid up for only three days. What else are you doing—supervising the farms? Ordering barns built? Directing my man of business?"

Trixy made to hit his hand away, to no avail. "Now you're being ridiculous," she accused, finally showing some sign of anger. "None of this was my idea. Let me go so that I can clean up the mess you've made with your childish temper, before the broth seeps entirely into the carpet."

Glynde's next words stopped her cold. "Oh, dear me—poor, poor Miss Beatrice Stourbridge. She didn't want any of this; none of this was her idea. It is true, then, madam, what Shakespeare wrote— that not all of us are born to greatness. Some of us, like you, poor thing, must have greatness thrust upon them." He gave her arm a small shake. "Did you really believe that I came down in the last rain, Trixy, that I should swallow such nonsense?"

Her eyes flashed emerald fire for a second—at the precise moment he had referred to her as Beatrice —before her lids came down, masking her expression. "I don't care a fig one way or the other what you believe, Harry," she told him quietly. "I hatched a plot—a terrible, flaw-riddled plot born of desperation—which failed almost immediately, stranding me in the middle of nowhere. Left with the twins to care for, and without another choice, I am now only following your orders, hopeful of ending this farce with the happy settlement of my charges and a few good prospects for future employment for myself."

Harry looked up at her, liking the faint color that filled her cheeks, enjoying the way her modestly covered breasts heaved in reaction to her obvious perturbation, feeling stirred by her proximity next to him on the bed. "Trixy, I—" he began, only to be cut off.

"It was not I who spooked Myles Somerville into running off to Ireland," she continued, unaware of his grace's change of mood from the angry to the amorous, "leaving his girls behind to fend for themselves. It was not I who had so little control of my hey-go-mad brother and his equally industrious bosom chum that they were left loose long enough to kidnap Eugenie and Helena. It was not I who hatched this absurd plan of your sponsoring the girls for the Season. It was not I who wouldn't listen to reason, but went skating off to play tricks on thin ice without so much as testing it beforehand. It was not I who took to my bed like some spoiled child, acting as if I were carrying the weight of the world upon my shoulders. It was not I who—"

"Oh, for the love of heaven, Trixy, shut up!" Harry exploded when he couldn't bear listening to her recital of his failings for another moment, and he dragged her down on top of him to put a halt to her protestations with his kiss.

11

IDIOT! SHE WAS AN IDIOT. There was no other word for it. How else could she describe herself? What other label could she—or anyone—put on a female who allowed a man, a near-stranger, actually, to kiss her? And in his own bed, for pity's sake. In his very own bed!

Trixy pushed the drawer shut on the last of her clothing and turned away from the armoire in disgust. Perhaps a better question would be: why was she still berating herself for that kiss three weeks later, with the whole lot of them finally installed in the Glynde mansion in Portman Square?

Indeed, why was she even continuing to think about it at all? Lord knew, Harry seemed to have forgotten the embrace had ever happened—or at least it certainly seemed that way.

Trixy perched on the edge of the bed, still having barely taken notice of her comfortable room, and relived yet again those terrible, wonderful moments in Harry's arms. It had not been her first kiss, for after all, she was not a child.

She had been kissed before—although perhaps Darryl Findley, the assistant curate at St. Hilda's, hadn't had quite the equivalent experience of the duke, whose kiss had certainly been as different from Darryl's hasty, sloppy clash of lips against teeth as was watered milk from thick, luscious cream.

No, Darryl had a lot to learn about kissing, if Harry's example was any indication of expertise in the exercise. Pressing a hand to her lips, her eyes closed, Trixy relived yet again the heady sensations that had exploded throughout her body as Harry had moved his mouth on hers.

Harry's mouth had been one thing—that greedy, searching, all-consuming, all-knowing mouth—but even more debilitating at the time had been the intimate press of his body against hers, his firm nightshirt-clad body, and the strength of his arms as they had held her to him.

Trixy jumped up from the bed to go to the single window that, because hers was one of the minor family chambers in the mansion, looked out over the mews, and stared at the scene outside without really seeing it, for her traitorous mind continued to insist upon concentrating on the scene in the Glyndevaron bedchamber.

Somehow, some way, she had to find a way to erase this dangerous memory from her mind.

During the day it was easy enough to do—almost as easy as it was to believe that she hated and detested Henry Lyle Augustus Townsend. His muttered curse and hasty dismissal of her as he had abruptly broken off the kiss was only one of the reasons why she should have had no trouble in banishing the man as well as the incident from her mind.

Not content with having humiliated her—for what else could his kiss have been if not a punishment for her audacity in saving him from drowning? (if she had it to do over again, she would stand on the shore waving her handkerchief at him and blowing kisses while watching him sink to the bottom of the pond like a stone)—he had risen from his sickbed that very day to, as he had announced at the time to all who would listen, "take back the reins of command before the enterprising Miss Stourbridge makes the lot of you believe she is indispensable."

From the moment of that sarcastic pronouncement, there had existed an undeclared state of war between Trixy and the duke—and so far, it appeared that the duke was winning.

Not yet fully recovered from his dousing in the pond, he had taken complete control of the plans for the Season with a vengeance, sticking his still-sniffling aristocratic nose into everything from the number of gowns each twin would need to exactly which simpering French dancing master should be employed to instruct the girls in the newly popular, though sometimes scandalously regarded waltz.

Once he had sent off the announcement to the newspapers telling of their expected official arrival date in the metropolis—which was set for exactly six weeks after they actually took up residence, leaving time for the modiste he had chosen to make up the wardrobes—Harry had figuratively doffed his cap to the lot of them and promptly departed for London and Angelo's roast beef.

Trixy liked to comfort herself with the notion that he had run away, unable to face her after what had passed between them in his chamber, but it was difficult to convince herself that, in truth, he had been affected by it at all. No, she couldn't make herself believe that Harry lay awake night after night weaving romantic fantasies, as she did. If he had run away in order to flee his memory of their embrace, it was because the mere thought of it disgusted him. Consider this: do men who find themselves suddenly besotted with a woman curse at the end of a kiss? Trixy thought it highly unlikely.

And what further proof did she need of his extreme disinterest than the fact that the traveling party had pulled up in Portman Square only to find that his grace, who had chanced upon a few friends passing through London on their way north, had joined them for a visit in Bury St. Edmunds and wasn't expected back until the very night of the ball he had planned for the twins' come-out.

Trixy leaned her forehead against the cold windowpane. "Six weeks until I see him again," she said quietly. "Six weeks of constant headaches, of outfitting Eugenie and Helena while trying to keep Andy and Willie from falling into every trap set for unwary, green-as-grass boys out on a spree, and six weeks of maintaining a delicate balance with Lady Amelia, who must continue to believe Harry is in love with me while understanding that this knowledge is to remain our particular secret. Added to that, I must cajole Angelo, keep Pinch from scaring off the newly hired servants, and somehow accomplish all the various chores Harry has left me on his abominable lists."

She turned away from the window with a heartfelt sigh. "If nothing else, by the time Harry finally finds his way back to Portman Square, I'll be too exhausted to be nervous about facing him again."

Six weeks. Harry slammed the lid shut on an array of rings and other masculine jewelry. Six weeks before he would look in Beatrice Stourbridge's soulful green eyes once more and see . . . what? Hatred? Disgust? Disdain? Hurt? Disillusionment?

He walked over to the bed and collapsed heavily onto the edge of it, cursing himself for having dismissed his valet. If his man were in the room he would not be able to allow his melancholy to show—which might be a good thing. It was better to keep busy, to keep moving, so that he had no time to think. No time to remember.

It had been the hurt in her eyes that had nearly destroyed him. He knew that now. The kiss—that damnable ill-timed, destructive, instructive, deliriously enjoyable kiss—had, he acknowledged, turned out to be the single most unintelligent action of his entire life.

It was not as if she were totally blameless in the affair, Harry had reminded himself more than once, for he was a man, and men have since time immemorial leavened their feelings of guilt with the sure knowledge that there exists no such creature as a totally innocent woman. He certainly had suffered mightily at Trixy Stourbridge's hands.

Even the most cruel judge would have to say that the duke's current situation—although rooted in his pursuit of Myles Somerville and generously fertilized by the chuckleheaded machinations of William and his harebrained cohort, Andrew—had only grown into a full-grown noxious weed patch when Trixy, with her threat of blackmail, had volunteered for the position of head gardener.

The duke stepped away from the bed and crossed to the large window that overlooked Lord Hargrove's weed-free east garden. "None of this is my fault, not really. I tried to avenge my father, just as any good son should. But when my attempt failed, did I become obsessed with thoughts of revenge? Did I go haring off to Ireland to confront Somerville? Did I even so much as entertain the thought of finding satisfaction in some other way— some terribly twisted way?

"No. I most certainly did not. I faced my disappointment like a man and went home, only to find that my beloved brother, in his innocence, had become the target of a ruthless blackmailer." The duke frowned as his last words hung in the air. They didn't sound quite right; quite fair. "Well, perhaps not exactly ruthless. 'Desperate' might be a better word." He chuckled softly. "Perhaps even 'inventive.'"

A lone horseman rode past below him, barely visible through the encroaching dusk that reminded him that it would soon be time for the dinner gong, and he retraced his steps to the jewelry box to select a plain gold signet ring that required no great sartorial decision-making on his part.

"Well, no matter what term I give it, I certainly spiked her guns soon enough," he consoled himself, thinking back on how he had turned the tables on Trixy, shattering her dreams of retiring to the country on his largess.

"If only she had let it go at that. But no," he said, jamming the ring onto his finger, "she couldn't do that, could she? She had to take over my household, make an idiot of me in front of my brother, and then hunt me down in my own chamber to tell me that she was an innocent party and I had brought all my troubles on myself. Kiss her? What a ridiculous reaction. I should have stuffed my pillow down her throat!"

His footsteps took him back to the window as his mind traveled, as had become its custom during moments of reflection, to that single heart-searing kiss he and Trixy had shared. Yes, they had shared the kiss. It may have been one-sided at its inception, but she had given as well as taken, her hands clutching at his shoulders, her soft breasts insinuating themselves against his chest.

How could such an exasperating woman still be such an intriguing, desirable creature? The duke couldn't understand it. Trixy was not exactly young, although, to be fair, she wasn't precisely ancient either. She hadn't come equipped with a handsome dowry, or been blessed with important connections. She certainly possessed none of the conventional claims to beauty. Why, he didn't even like red hair, now that he thought about the thing. Red, as far as he was concerned, looked good only on Irish setters! It was just, it was just that . . .

"I don't know what it just is!" the duke exclaimed in exasperation, pressing his heated forehead against the cool windowpane. "Dammit! It just is!"

His head still resting against the windowpane, Glynde faced his biggest problem. "Six weeks until the night of the ball. Six weeks until I see her again. How will she look? How will I act? Will she goad me into disgracing myself again? Will I be able to keep my hands off her? Six weeks. Am I doomed to thinking of her for every moment of that time? How will I stand it? Even more to the point, how will anyone stand me?"

Sighing, he turned away from the window just as Sir Roderick Hilliard entered the room without bothering to knock, unknowingly finishing off Glynde's thoughts about the impact of his recent melancholia on his friends.

"Harry! I've run you to ground at last. Are you coming down? I have to tell you, friend, you have not exactly been the most congenial fellow all week. Salty says you're casting a damp shadow over the whole party, and I'm beginning to think he's right, which bothers me most extremely, for you know how I loathe agreeing with Salty about anything. It's not like you, Harry. Not like you at all."

Sir Roderick's mention of Grover Saltaire's remarks goaded Glynde into snapping, at least momentarily, out of his doldrums—and into a spur-of-the-moment stroke of what he sincerely hoped was genius.

"Roddy," he improvised swiftly, stepping smartly toward the door, "have I told you that I've taken on the chore of launching some young friends of my aunt's this Season? They're twins, you know—young, blond, pretty as buttercups, and as alike in looks as two peas in a pod." He slipped one arm companionably about Sir Roderick's broad shoulders. "Now, seeing as how I'm rather new at this come-out business—a sad lack that has kept me worrying and fretting all week—and seeing as how you and Salty are two of my oldest and dearest friends—"

"Twins, you say?" Sir Roderick interrupted, falling into step with the duke—as well as into Glynde's hands, although the handsome peer was, thankfully, blissfully unaware of that fact. It was enough that Harry had surprisingly lumped him and Salty together under the title of "dearest friends," a level of intimacy Sir Roderick hadn't known he had with the duke. "Do they have any portion? Not that I'm purse-pinched or anything like that."

Glynde laughed, knowing that neither Sir Roderick nor Grover had to look to marriage as a way out of oppressing debt. "Did the Gunnings have need of a portion, Roddy?"

"The Gunnings?" Sir Roderick lifted a hand to stroke at his short black beard. "I've seen portraits of those two, you know. As pretty as all that, are they? Tell me, Harry—seeing as how I helped my aunt pop off m'sister Charlotte last year—do you think it would make you less uneasy if Salty and I joined you in town for the ball, being your dearest friends and all?"

Glynde would not have to face Trixy alone. He would have his "friends" by his side, to guide him, to help him, to protect him. His smile was so wide it nearly gave the game away. "Why, Roddy, how kind of you—and what a splendid idea. Now I can relax and enjoy myself, knowing everything will be just fine. How can I ever thank you?"

Sir Roderick shrugged his wide shoulders. "Don't say another word about it, Harry. Just think a minute—what else are friends for, if they can't help one another? Now, let's go ferret out Salty and give him the good news."

They walked down the wide hallway arm in arm, in search of Grover Saltaire, Harry's second intended victim. "Twins, you say," Sir Roderick repeated thoughtfully. "Yes, I think Salty and I will have a jolly good time helping you out, Harry. A jolly good time."

A spring once more in his step, and with his heart feeling pounds lighter than it had, Glynde purposefully cleared his mind of any thoughts of a certain red-haired "problem" and, as Sir Roderick pounded heavily on Grover Saltaire's chamber door, dedicated himself to enjoying the coming six weeks to the top of his bent, and the devil take the hindmost!

It is widely known that when it comes to the more ticklish dilemmas of romance, men—including the Duke of Glynde—do not experience much difficulty in deluding themselves with the hope that studiously ignoring their troubling situation, and enlisting as allies other men as blithely ignorant as themselves, will sooner or later result in the romantic problem solving itself.

This optimistic conclusion, when coupled with the likewise widely known fact that women do not take this same ostrichlike view, probably accounts for the fact that so very, very many men do eventually wake up one fine morning to discover themselves married.

12

THE MANSION IN PORTMAN SQUARE had been a veritable beehive of activity from cellar to attic for nearly every moment of the previous six weeks, but if the number of carriages now vying for space outside the Glynde front door was any indicator, the twins' come-out ball—if not their entire Season—was bound to be a roaring success.

"Or at least it will be a success among those members of society most likely to dine out on gossip," Trixy told her reflection in the drawing-room mirror before hastening out of the room, on her way to join Lady Amelia at the top of the landing outside the ballroom. "Tongues will be wagging all over Mayfair tomorrow when it gets out that the esteemed Duke of Glynde couldn't bother to show up at his own ball—the rat!"

"A rat, am I? With beady eyes and one of those long, straight tails? Oh, unkind! Unkind! And after all I've done for you, Miss Stourbridge? I have to confess it, you have cut me to the quick."

Trixy halted in her tracks and whirled about to

see none other than the supposedly absent Duke of Glynde, large as life, lounging at his ease against a thick marble pillar in the hallway. He was clad in splendidly cut midnight-blue evening clothes, his snowy white cravat accenting his tanned skin that flattered his casually arranged dark locks, sparkling, even white teeth, and gray eyes. He was gorgeous.

Trixy's stomach—and all her hard-won resolve of the last six weeks—immediately turned craven and promptly plummeted straight to her toes.

She blurted into speech. "Harry! You've come back. Why wasn't I told?"

"Why weren't you told?" Glynde pushed himself away from the pillar, his smile melting beneath a mighty scowl. "And why should you be? My aunt was informed of my arrival two hours ago, as she is a beloved member of my family—as well as my hostess. I have taken Somerville's brats as temporary wards—making them my family of sorts, I suppose, now that I think on it, so that I may have been remiss by not alerting them to my return as well—but I have to own it, madam, I do not remember ever adopting you. It's amazing, but I had almost forgotten how encroaching you can be. It was very kind of you to remind me."

Trixy raised her chin and took two slow steps in the duke's direction, then stopped to stare up at him most intently.

He hadn't noticed her pale seafoam-green gown, a beauteous creation she had thanked Lady Amelia for at least seven dozen times since its purchase.

He hadn't noticed her newly styled upswept hair,

or the delicate strands of faux pearls that the hair-dresser had twined so cleverly through her burnished curls.

He hadn't noticed, as she herself couldn't help but notice—considering that she had stopped before every mirror in the mansion on her way to the ball-room, to reassure herself that the mirror in her bed-chamber had not been lying to her—that she had never been in better looks.

And, most important of all, it was clear as glass that he most certainly had no intention of bringing up the matter of their last meeting and the embrace they had shared. Oh, no. Harry was much, much too busy finding new ways to insult her to notice or mention anything at all.

Had she ever really believed herself vulnerable to this smug, insufferable man? Had she ever actually considered that her heart could be in danger once he deigned to return to London? Had she ever, even in her wildest dreams, felt the least bit guilty about trying her hand at blackmailing a duke?

Now, Trixy Stourbridge was by nature slow to anger. What else could explain her willingness to put up with the many terrible positions she'd had since her father's demise—including this last trouble-ridden sojourn with the *les deux* Somerville? Trixy was the last person to be mean, or petty, or to allow herself to be slighted when, indeed, no slight was intended. Really she was. But then, up until this moment at least, Trixy had always believed herself to be heart-whole.

Her jaw hardened. Harry had intended this slight.

He had seen her and then purposely ignored her altered appearance. She knew it. She could feel it deep in every fiber of her being. Duke or no, Harry Townsend was a man, and he was acting just like a man—nasty! If she felt no *tendre* for him, she doubted she could be this angry with him. But she did feel something for him, and he knew it, drat him!

She had, as she saw it, two choices open to her at this point in time. One, she could launch herself at him, scratch his adorable grinning face, and then stomp out of the mansion—and straight into penniless oblivion. Or, two, she could stand her ground, swallow her pride, and bide her time until she, the woman who cared for him, found a way to make the Duke of Glynde's life a miserable, never-ending hell!

Trixy was silent for some time, long moments during which Glynde's lamentably easy-to-read eyes looked unwaveringly into her own. His entire expression was one of amusement, liberally laced with masculine condescension and something else that Trixy could only interpret as relief.

A slight quivering of his lips, as if he were holding back a laugh, sealed his fate.

Slowly and quite distinctly, Trixy said at last, "Please forgive my impertinence, your grace. I am, after all, only an employee, and a temporary employee at that. Of course you are not obliged to inform me of your comings and goings. Your instructions have been carried out to the letter, your grace, by the way—save for one small problem. Because you are bringing out twins, we have no idea how to start off the ball, as you cannot possibly lead both Helena and Eugenie into the first set of dances. I will say that Helena has become much the better dancer, spending long hours receiving extra instruction from the teacher you ordered provided, but that is not really a good answer, is it? Perhaps you have a suggestion?"

As Trixy spoke, any hint of humor left Glynde's face, to be replaced by a look of confused consternation that had her toes curling in delight. Her aching heart eased. He did have some affection for her. He had to. Otherwise he wouldn't care one way or the other how his words, his slights, affected her.

She would be magnanimous. She would, for the moment, let bygones be bygones, banishing the memory of their last awkward meeting in favor of planning for the future.

Trixy had, at the outset, thought only to make Lady Amelia believe Harry was interested in her— her single intention being to get a little of her own back for his insulting remark about finding herself a widower with a large brood to wed. Now the entire complexion of the matter had changed. She had changed. His kiss had changed her. Now she would settle for nothing less than his love.

"Harry?" she inquired, tilting her head to one side because he hadn't answered her question. "Carriages are beginning to arrive in the square, and we must make our way to the ballroom. Do you have a solution to our problem or not?"

"What, ho, Harry?" came a bellow from the stairs. "And who could this ravishing creature be,

I ask? Never tell me she is one of the twins, for you promised me they were blond angels. This one looks more earthly than heaven-sent, but gorgeous nonetheless. Introduce me, man, so that I might kiss that dainty hand."

Trixy looked toward the staircase to see a tall, dark-haired, bearded gentleman lightly descending to join them. Beards were not really in vogue, Trixy knew, and most probably hadn't been since the days of Sir Walter Raleigh, but she could readily see why the gentleman had adopted the affectation. He looked mysterious and somehow dashing, although she would privately wager that the thing had to be dreadfully uncomfortable in the summertime.

"Trixy," Harry said as the gentleman stopped in front of her, eyeing her, or so she thought, as if she were the prize in some raffle, "please allow me to introduce to you Sir Roderick Hilliard. Roddy, make your bow to Miss Stourbridge, companion to Misses Eugenie and Helena Somerville."

"Madam, your most devoted servant," Sir Roderick announced, placing a kiss on the back of her hand, the slight scrape of his beard forcing her to suppress the urge to rub at her skin to banish the tickling sensation it had caused.

Sir Roderick turned to Glynde. "Harry, old man, for shame. You've been holding out on us. Simpering little misses, indeed. I'll leave them to you and Salty, and take Miss Stourbridge, if you don't mind. I always was partial to redheads." He turned back to Trixy. "M'mother was a redhead, you know. Lovely, sainted woman. Dead now, of course. I miss her terribly."

"Roddy," Harry interrupted, an edge to his voice that delighted Trixy, "leave off, won't you, before you have me blubbering and Miss Stourbridge succumbing to sympathy over your loss. Your sainted mother's been dead for well over twenty years. Besides, I've seen her portrait. Her hair was as black as a crow's."

Sir Roderick gave a dismissive wave of his hand. "Details, my boy. Merely details. She always seemed like a redhead—fiery, you know. Are you fiery, Miss Stourbridge?"

"What I am, Sir Roderick," Trixy responded with a smile, "is in a terrible rush—as you should be, Harry. Pinch can't hold back the descending hordes forever, you know, and we cannot leave Lady Amelia alone to greet your guests." So saying, she dropped a small curtsy in the gentlemen's general direction and headed for the ballroom.

Harry caught up with her in less than a moment. "I've decided what we will do about the first dance," he said, grabbing Sir Roderick's arm so that the man was dragged along with them whether he liked it or not. "Roddy here will lead out Helena, and Salty—another gentleman I've brought with me— can squire Eugenie."

Trixy turned her head to eye the duke warily. "And just where will you be, Harry, while your friends stand in for you? Propping up some pillar? And just who, pray tell, is this Salty person? With a name like that, he might not be acceptable to your aunt."

"Grover Saltaire is his given name," Sir Roderick informed her, neatly slipping her left hand around his elbow as they mounted the staircase to the ballroom. "He's the best of all good fellows— although, come to think of it, I don't remember him as much of a prancer. Maybe you should rethink the thing, Harry—considering Miss Eugenie's toes."

In the end, the duke's original plan was adopted, thanks both to his adamant refusal to do more than formally introduce the Somerville girls as the guests passed through the receiving line and to Grover Saltaire's eager acceptance of the arrangement once he had clapped eyes on the beauteous Eugenie.

Two hours later, and the ball, the first given at the Glynde mansion in over a decade, was already a rousing success, thanks mostly to Lady Amelia's lavish use of pink bunting and orchids in a decorating scheme to rival those of Prinny himself. The orchestra was in top form, and the guests, as it was early in the Season and they had not yet had a chance to acquire the necessary *ennui* usually so visible at *ton* affairs, crowded the floor for every set.

Trixy, who had not yet danced—and did not expect to dance, although she certainly might have hoped to take the floor at least once—stood to one side of the ballroom, keeping her eyes on Helena, who seemed rather downcast even though she had not lacked for partners the entire evening.

Eugenie, on the other hand, was very animated, laughing and talking and generally appearing as if she had been born to be the center of attention— which both she and her sister appeared to be, as their dance cards had filled almost before the end of the first set.

Grover Saltaire seemed a splendid choice for Eugenie, as the two physically perfect blonds made a striking couple as they went down the dance—and Trixy had been forced to scratch the man's name out twice on Eugenie's dance card or else the whole town would have them betrothed by morning. As it was, Eugenie was engaged to go down to supper with the man.

Trixy frowned, dismissing Eugenie from her mind and looking over the crowd once more to seek out Helena. She located the girl easily enough, dancing with an older gentleman who was showing all the signs of making a regular cake of himself, trying to keep up with the steps of an energetic Scottish reel. Trixy hid a smile behind her gloved hand as the man tripped on his sash and nearly tumbled to the floor, but her smile faded as Helena stopped dead, heaved her slim shoulders in a mighty sigh, and then continued on gracefully, her own smile small and wan.

"Not dancing, Miss Stourbridge? Surely it can't be because of any lack of offers."

Trixy gave Helena one last look, then turned to see Sir Roderick standing beside her. "I am only a companion, Sir Roderick," she pointed out, determinedly stilling her left foot, which had been tapping in time to the music, "and am not expected to dance. As a matter of fact, I am most probably breaking some unwritten law by standing here, and should be sitting primly alongside all those turbaned dowagers over there who are enjoying themselves mightily by verbally tearing apart the reputation of everyone else in the place."

"Nonsense," Sir Roderick said, placing a hand on

her elbow and guiding her out onto the floor. "I have performed all my duty dances and I demand a reward in the form of a turn around this great barn with the most beautiful woman in the room. It's only fair, seeing as how I helped you and Harry out by squiring that die-away Helena Somerville twice. Is the child sickening for something, do you think? I never met such a maudlin miss."

Her concern for Helena overpowering her reluctance to put herself on show when she knew very well that Harry would have something nasty and cutting to say about it later, Trixy automatically moved into the steps of the dance, asking, "So you saw it too? What do you suppose could be the problem? Helena is usually quite cheerful. Perhaps I should go to her."

"Leaving me behind, devastated, my heart shattered? I should think not, Miss Stourbridge. Besides, we are in the middle of a dance. You can hardly haul the child off the floor, demanding to know why she isn't grinning, now, can you?"

Trixy smiled up at the man, liking his beard more each time she saw it. "A broken heart, Sir Roderick? Over me? Why, if I didn't know better, I'd say you were flirting with me."

The movement of the dance brought them close together. "I do know better, Miss Stourbridge, and I do believe I am flirting with you. Tell me, would you like to go driving with me in the park tomorrow afternoon? I have a new phaeton I'm longing to try out in the promenade. My new geldings come from Tatt's, so you know they are supreme."

Trixy hesitated, knowing that she could never

picture Sir Roderick as anything more than a friend. But just then the sound of a trilling laugh reached her ears and she turned to see Glynde engaged in lighthearted banter with a glorious brunette whose gown left few of her charms to the imagination. "I'd love to take a ride in the park, Sir Roderick," she said, deliberately batting her eyelashes at the man. "As a matter of fact, I can think of nothing I should enjoy more."

13

IT HAD NEARLY gone four in the morning before the last of the guests staggered out onto the flagway and Trixy could shoo the girls upstairs to bed, Eugenie chattering nineteen to the dozen about the handsome, charming Grover Saltaire and Helena still strangely subdued.

Lady Amelia, still fanning herself with a huge ostrich-plume fan that had suffered a prodigious workout throughout the length of the evening, announced that "we are a brilliant success" as she, too, climbed the staircase, Pinch at her elbow to assist her in the ascent.

Andy, who had spent most of the evening standing about in the card room, watching as Lord Halsey dropped more than five hundred pounds without a blink, was explaining the fine points of some card game to Willie as the two followed in Lady Amelia's wake, Willie, like Helena, uncharacteristically subdued.

Harry, Trixy noticed as she lingered in the black-and-white-tile foyer, was nowhere to be seen.

She wandered back into the ballroom to send the yawning servants to bed, telling them they could finish their work in the morning, and then went about snuffing candles that were threatening to sputter out by themselves.

It was strange how forlorn the ballroom looked to her now, devoid of people. The pink bunting, which had seemed so romantic only a few hours earlier, now just looked tired, and seemed to sag in all the wrong places. The flowers had already begun to wilt, and the rows of empty chairs, once arranged so precisely, looked like the broken lines of weary soldiers hastily reassembled after a fierce battle.

Trixy had danced only a single time, with Sir Roderick, since no other man had approached her all evening. Not that she was too disappointed. She hadn't really expected to become the belle of the ball, although she had, deep in her heart of hearts, hoped that Harry might have—

Trixy bit her lip, purposefully banishing the traitorous thought from her mind. Lady Amelia, bless her, had sidled up to Trixy halfway through the evening to explain that Harry very rarely danced, which wasn't to say that he had lost interest in her, which Lady Amelia was sure he hadn't, for Trixy looked very sweet in her gown and Harry wasn't, after all, a blind man.

Walking to the center of the ballroom, Trixy shook her head as she remembered Lady Amelia's words. The woman had taken a liking to Trixy, as Trixy had to her, and she did not look forward to viewing Lady Amelia's eventual inevitable disappointment when the end of the Season came.

One dance. Was that really too much to ask from the man? One single dance. A waltz, perhaps. Yes . . . yes, definitely a waltz.

Trixy slipped a finger into the small fabric loop positioned halfway down the skirt of her gown and lifted the material as she would have if she were going to dance the waltz. Her left hand went out to rest lightly on the shoulder of her imaginery partner and her eyes closed as she listened to the music playing inside her head.

Slowly, hesitantly, she began to dance. One, two, three . . . one, two, three. Standing nearly on tiptoe in her soft satin slippers, she moved around the floor, her steps growing more confident as her body dipped and swayed and twirled and her seafoam-green gown floated above the floor.

One, two, three . . . one, two, three. How she loved the waltz. How graceful it was, how exhilarating, how potentially dangerous.

Suddenly she was no longer dancing alone. Without warning, she had a partner, a gloriously graceful partner who whisked her around the perimeter of the floor as if the pair of them were dancing on clouds. No, her brain screamed at her, this couldn't be true. She must be imagining it. She must be imagining the fingers cradling hers, as well as the hand that pressed lightly against the small of her back.

Her eyes opened wide in shock, yet her feet continued to move in time with the silent melody of the dance. "Harry!" She breathed his name more than spoke it. "What—"

He smiled down on her almost benevolently before sweeping her into another turn. "Forgive me, Trixy, but I couldn't resist. You looked very appealing gliding around the floor, but you really did need a partner to make the picture complete. What waltz are we dancing, by the way? Perhaps I could hum along?"

Trixy tore herself from his light embrace, turning away from him. "Poor duke," she said, her heart bitter. "Was there nothing else to amuse you this late in the evening, so that you had to settle for sticking pins in me? Perhaps you should go wake Andy and Willie—they might want to help you prop a coffin at someone's front door, or some other such prank."

Glyndé might not have had as much experience in dealing with the gentler sex as some of his cohorts, but he was likewise no green-as-grass youth, and he immediately recognized the fact that Trixy was upset with him. Reaching out to halt her escape by grabbing hold of her arm, he said, "I wasn't trying to amuse myself with you, Trixy. Maybe I was, once, but not now—and not for some time."

She turned back to face him. Was he referring to their kiss at Glyndevaron? Had it really meant something to him, something important? She had to know. "Meaning . . . ?"

Harry shook his head, running a hand through his hair in obvious agitation. "Meaning . . . ? What is it about females, anyway? Meaning what? Why must they have everything set out for them in neat little blocks? Can't you just take a man's word for anything? Must we always explain?"

Harry looked so sweet in his confusion that Trixy was hard-pressed not to retract her question, but then she remembered how shabbily he had treated her earlier in the evening—how shabbily he had been treating her ever since they had first met. Why should she make anything easier for him? He certainly had not gone out of his way to smooth any of life's wrinkles for her!

And so she continued to stand her ground, looking up at him levelly, waiting for him to speak.

The duke remained silent for some time, knowing that whatever he said next could return to haunt him for years to come. The dratted woman knew he was attracted to her—he could tell from the smug, self-satisfied look on her face. She also knew, he was certain, that he had enjoyed kissing her—and wanted to repeat the experience.

Well, Harry considered further, if she knew all that, there was really no point in prolonging the thing, now, was there? No, there certainly was not. She knew how he felt, yet she wasn't running from him. Obviously she wanted him as much as he wanted her. At least she was being honest about the thing. You had to admire a woman who was honest about such things.

All that was left now was to put thought into action.

Snaking out a hand to grab her forearm, Harry pulled Trixy fully into his arms and brought his mouth down hard on hers. The flame he had felt ignite at their first kiss immediately accelerated into a conflagration as her pliant body molded against his own. Her mouth was so soft, so wondrously enticing, that he forgot to go slowly, convinced himself that there was no need to be gentle. His lips slanted first one way, then the other, as he boldly invaded her mouth to taste the sweetness within.

It was only when his hand, moving almost without orders from him, sought her breast, that Trixy pulled away, leaving him on the very edge of frustration.

"What's wrong, love?" he asked, desperately trying to control the tremor in his arms as he pulled her back against his chest. "Don't tell me you didn't enjoy that as much as I did, for we both know it would be a lie. Your reaction confused me the first time, but I've been thinking the whole thing over for the last six weeks, and I've finally figured it out—figured you out. You aren't in this just for a kiss, are you? You want more. We're so right for each other, Trixy. I think I've known it since the first moment I saw you, and so did you. There's no reason to fight it anymore."

Trixy allowed her taut muscles to relax as she leaned against Harry's strength. He was right. What was she fighting for, anyway? She had been attracted to him from the beginning, had been dreaming of a moment like this for the past six weeks and more.

She was no child, no simpering miss. Her reaction to his first kiss had been childish and immature. Harry's kiss tonight had told her that he returned her feelings. The impossible fairy tale she had dreamed of all those long years past was at last coming true.

Michelle Kasey

"Oh, Harry," she murmured passionately, reaching up her arms to slip them around his shoulders, "we're going to be so very happy."

He bent his head to nuzzle at the soft skin behind her ear. "Yes, love, we will be very happy. We'll have to get through the Season somehow, now that I've gone so far as to commit Aunt Amelia to the project, but I'm sure we'll have the twins settled in no time. That's still part of the bargain, isn't it? Yes, I'm sure it is, for if nothing else, love, you're an honorable blackmailer. Then, my darling, I can feel free to set you up somewhere—somewhere close to Glyndevaron, so that I can see you whenever I want. That will be very often, I'm sure."

Trixy, her head still tilted to one side as Harry's lips caressed her throat, making a mockery of her senses, felt her insides slowly turning to stone. "Set me up somewhere, Harry? What do you mean?" She set her palms against his chest and pushed him away. "You want to make me your mistress?"

Harry frowned at the brittle edge to Trixy's tone. "Why, yes—what did you think I meant? That's what you wanted from the outset, wasn't it? An allowance and a place in the country? That was the payment you planned to exact from me. That was why you reacted as you did to my first kiss. You thought I was trying to get something for nothing. At first I thought you were insulted, or hurt, but it was only business, wasn't it, and you wanted me to figure out that you still planned to hold out for the cottage.

"But your plan worked, even if you hadn't figured on developing a romantic attachment. Naughty puss. You'll still have your cottage and allowance—I give them both to you as of this moment. The only difference now is that you'll have me there as well."

A single tear spilled onto Trixy's cheek.

"Oh . . . I see," Harry said, his gaze sliding away from hers. "No! No, wait a moment. I don't see, dammit! You never thought I was . . . that *we* would . . . but I never *said* . . . I never thought . . . you couldn't . . . but you *do*! It seems I underestimated you. You really did plan to fly high, didn't you? But that's going too far, puss. I mean, you tried to blackmail me. You threatened to bring shame down on my family.

"You're a woman of the world, an intelligent, enterprising woman. Why, you've probably entered into just such an arrangement as I've suggested before—maybe more than once. Surely you didn't think that we'd . . . You wouldn't even want us to . . . Just what sort of a rig are you trying to run now? What's the matter, Trixy? Has this bit of *ton* life brought out new demands to add to your old ones?"

"Don't be silly. Of course I understood what you were offering, Harry, and I wouldn't be so mean as to change my demands in the middle of the game," Trixy said quickly, before Harry's damning words could totally destroy her and force her to her knees, whimpering. "I just wanted to be perfectly clear on the terms you were offering. A house in the country, I believe you said, and an allowance—just what I had originally demanded? How much of an allowance? You were partially correct—I have learned to enjoy living and dressing well. And how often would I be expected to . . . to entertain you?"

Harry was beginning to experience the sinking feeling that he had blundered, and blundered badly—only he wasn't quite sure how. Her eyes were overbright, for one thing, and now that he really thought about it, Trixy didn't seem the sort to enjoy being a kept woman. "Look, Trixy, if I've said something wrong—"

"Said something wrong?" she interrupted brightly, patting his cheek. "How could you have possibly said something wrong? I'm a blackmailer, pure and simple. Heaven knows you've reminded me of that fact often enough.

"There's only one thing, Harry," Trixy pointed out, backing away toward the doorway. "Sir Roderick seemed to be rather taken with me tonight, and I wouldn't want to jeopardize my chance for a more—shall we say—permanent position, if you take my meaning. After all, you yourself hinted that I should do my best to land myself a husband while I'm chaperoning the girls, didn't you?"

Harry took a step in her direction, frowning as she then backed up another two steps. "Well, yes, I suppose I did say something like that once, but . . . Roddy?" He spread his arms, smiling. "You're attracted to me, Trixy—not Roddy."

"True. I have to admit, this mutual attraction we feel is quite tempting. But business is still business, as I'm sure you understand. For now, I shall only say yes to the cottage and allowance, my original demands. The rest we shall leave up to fate," Trixy concluded swiftly, turning for the door as a second tear threatened to betray her. "Good night, Harry. Please be sure to snuff out the rest of the candles. It wouldn't do to burn the place to the ground."

A moment later Harry was alone in the ballroom, trying to figure out when he had first sensed that he had lost control of their strange conversation. He was sure Trixy had lied to him about misconstruing his proposition for a proposal. She wouldn't have cried otherwise. But marriage? The whole idea was ludicrous! To be honest, the thought of marriage to Beatrice Stourbridge, pretty though she might be, intelligent though she might be, attracted to her though he might be, had never entered his head. Running tame in his household must be giving her delusions of grandeur.

Women like Trixy weren't for marrying—they were for bedding, repeatedly, until it was time to move on to the next willing partner. Surely she knew that, just as surely as she knew dukes didn't marry nobodies—especially not nobodies that tried to blackmail them, for pity's sake. He would become a laughingstock if he were to marry Trixy.

Wasn't it bad enough that he had been maneuvered into sponsoring Myles Somerville's offspring for the Season? He knew that many of his guests tonight had been laughing behind his back at the absurdity of the thing—not that any of them would dare to say anything to his face. That, he reminded himself, was another injury he could lay squarely at Trixy's door. A laughingstock? Why, if all the truth were ever to come out, he'd have to change his name and scurry off to India or somewhere to live down the shame of the thing.

Marry her? At the moment, Harry wasn't even quite sure he still wanted Trixy as his mistress. She'd been no end of trouble already. Once he had set her up in her own cottage, she would most probably prove to be the most demanding creature in nature. Actually, he decided, taking up the snuffer to begin putting out the remaining candles, he had most probably just had a very lucky escape. Yes, that was how he would look at the thing—as a very lucky escape. Let Sir Roderick deal with Trixy if he was so entranced with her.

"Roddy?" Harry questioned aloud, shaking his head as he walked out of the darkened ballroom. "She must be serious about business being business. How else could she possibly prefer that bearded nincompoop to me?"

14

THE WEEK FOLLOWING the twins' come-out ball
was, to say the least, hectic. To say the most, it was
seven days and nights so chock-full of bustle from
dawn to nearly dawn again that it was no wonder
that events and places and things were concen-
trated upon almost without exception, leaving the
various souls of Glynde mansion little free time in
which to think about anything save their own
particular problems.

Trixy was perhaps the most preoccupied
inhabitant of the mansion, and not without reason.
If she had found it difficult to reconcile herself to
the idea of being a reluctant blackmailer, the notion
of being considered mistress material had all but
shocked her into speechlessness.

As she had relived that last embarrassing
conversation between herself and the duke—and
she relived it almost hourly, much to her disgust—
she had at last come to the conclusion that she had
handled herself quite well under the circumstances,
while the best she could say about Harry's part in

the whole affair was that he had behaved with all the finesse of a greased pig attempting to navigate its way along a tightrope strung fifty feet above a sty.

All right, so her heart had been broken—stomped on, actually, until it had been pounded into a million tiny painful pieces. Was this such an unusual occurrence among penniless ladies with no prospects, who dared to dream of happily-ever-after with the wealthy, titled men of their dreams? No, it was not. It was so ordinary, as a matter of fact, so totally predictable, that Trixy could only wonder that she had ever been so foolish as to have dared to dream of such unremitting bliss in the first place.

She had dared to dream, and made a sad hash of the thing. However, she had also dared to blackmail—and once again, that part of her plan seemed to be coming along swimmingly, as Eugenie and Helena had been pursued by more than a dozen suitors each ever since the ball.

Not only that, but Trixy's plan to revenge herself on the duke for all his many slights had been growing by leaps and bounds, even though she had stopped personally applying herself to the task from the moment she had used Sir Roderick's interest in her as a cutting exit line to get her out of harm's way before she betrayed her true feelings for Harry.

Sir Roderick, bless the man, had taken up the slack nicely, paying her court daily, taking her out on drives, sending her flowers, standing up with her at dances, and generally, by his devotion, driving his friend the duke all but round the bend.

It was all gratifying in the extreme to watch, because Harry, Trixy was sure, was caught between the urge to tell Sir Roderick the truth about her—effectively destroying the relationship—and what she hoped was an equally compelling urge to punch the neatly bearded man squarely on the nose because he was, she sincerely prayed, extremely jealous.

He *was* jealous. Trixy was sure of it. He did want her. She was equally sure of that. The single bright spot in the entire mess remained the knowledge that he had admitted to wanting her. But he would no sooner contemplate marriage with her than he would consider jumping from the White Tower in an effort to launch himself to the moon.

And that's why Trixy was so unhappy in the midst of the captivating frenzy of the Season, and why she could only hope with every fiber of her being that the twins would soon be settled so that she could tuck her tail between her legs and slink off somewhere to lick her many wounds.

As Trixy stood in front of a full-length mirror in her bedchamber just after luncheon, her heart not really in the thing as she considered whether her simple strand of garnets really was appropriate adornment for the gown she had chosen for that evening's entertainment at Lady Hereford's, Lacy knocked on the door and, not being bidden to enter, entered anyway.

"And there ye be, missy, primpin' and plannin' ta take yerself out struttin' again, without so much as a single thought ta m'poor babies."

Trixy looked at the maid's reflection as she saw

it in the mirror—or at least she saw part of it, for Lacy was a very large woman and much of her bulk did not fit within the gilt frame. "Your poor babies, Lacy? When last I saw Helena and Eugenie, they were off to Bond Street with Lady Amelia to look at hats. What's wrong?"

The maid jammed her fists onto her ample hips. "As if ye didn't know," she countered, sniffing. "Helena's moonin' around like her best chum just up and left her, and m'darlin' Eugenie is ridin' fer a fall, moonin' over that Salty fella."

Trixy moved away from the mirror to sit on the edge of the bed. "Let's take this one step at a time, if you please, Lacy. First of all, I have noticed that Helena isn't quite entering into the thrill of the Season with all the joy I could have wished. At first I thought it was because Willie wasn't paying her enough attention, but the boy is clearly besotted with her. Does Helena believe Harry—I mean, the duke—will cut up stiff at the match?"

"Lord Willie?" the maid said with a sniff. "That's yesterday's news, missy, and ye'd know it well enough if you was paying any attention ta anythin' but yerself. There'll be no match in that quarter, and no mistake. The colleen likes Lord Willie well enough, and he's a fine broth of a boy for all he did truss me up like a chicken that first night, but the wind's blowin' in another quarter altogether nowadays, if ye can take m'meanin'."

Trixy put a hand to her head, wondering if Lady Amelia would object overmuch if she tried to cry off for the evening, complaining of the headache. Didn't she have enough on her mind without having to deal with another of Helena's infatuations? Besides, Harry wasn't going to be at Lady Hereford's, a fact he had made very clear earlier as they sat around the table at luncheon. "And from which quarter would the wind be blowing today, Lacy?"

Lacy rolled her eyes and plopped her ample body down in a nearby chair. "And if I knew that, missy, would I be needin' ye? Whoever he is, he's makin' m'baby unhappy, and when I finds him I'll make him smell hell for that!"

"I'm sure you will, Lacy," Trixy said, privately believing that Helena's latest infatuation would prove to be as short-lived as any of the half-dozen that had come before it. "In the meantime, I promise to watch her closely, all right?"

"And what are ye goin' ta do about Eugenie, hmm?" the maid persisted. "Floatin' above the ground, the dear, daft child is, head over ears in love with this Mr. Grover Saltaire of hers. Lunatic sort of name, don't ya think?"

Trixy was fast losing interest in the conversation, as she considered it much too early in the game for either of the twins to be on the verge of marriage. "Lunatic? Oh, you mean 'Grover,' don't you?"

" 'Grover'? No, of course not. I meant 'Saltaire.' Silly name, don't you know." Lacy lifted a hand to pat at her hair. "Says she'll be takin' me with her when she weds, Eugenie does, as there ain't no one she loves so much as me. She didn't mention you, o'course, but then, ye already took care of settlin' yerself with a cottage and a pocketful of ill-gotten money, didn't ye, now, even before ye was sure about the girls. No, there ain't no one she loves so much as me."

"I'm sure there isn't," Trixy agreed wearily, rising to return to her station in front of the mirror and another inspection of the garnet necklace. She might as well have the word "blackmailer" branded on her forehead. Didn't anyone understand that she had only thought the scheme up on the spur of the moment, and was not a dedicated thief? No, she supposed not.

She brought herself back to the subject at hand. "So you think Mr. Saltaire is only toying with Miss Eugenie's affections? Perhaps you're right, Lacy, as he is, after all, a friend of the duke's. I will have a talk with her."

Lacy hauled herself to her feet. "Ye don't pay a body a whole lot of attention these days, do ye, missy? I didn't say this Salty fella is leadin' Eugenie down the garden path. That ain't it a'tall. It's the mother, the good Lord blight all meddlin' mamas. She's the one what's makin' all the trouble, cuttin' up stiff at the match. My little darlin' thinks she'll wear the besom down in time, but not ta m'way o'thinkin', she won't. No, no."

Trixy felt herself becoming angry. It was one thing for Harry to see her as beneath him—for, after all, he was a duke—but it was quite another matter for Grover Saltaire's mother to look down her not-so-noble nose at Eugenie, whose own mother, after all, had been second cousin to the Earl of Pembroke!

"Eugenie really loves Mr. Saltaire?" she asked,

her green eyes narrowing to slits as she glared into the mirror.

"Fit to die," the maid answered firmly, crossing her arms over her ample bosom.

"And Mr. Saltaire returns her affections?"

"And would she be wearin' his ring round her neck on a ribbon long enough ta keep the thing hidden beneath her nightshift iffen he didn't, that's what I want to know."

Trixy turned to face the maid. "You're right, Lacy. This could prove serious. I'll see what I can do, starting tonight at Lady Hereford's. We must make sure Eugenie doesn't feel herself forced to do something rash. We don't want her marrying over the anvil."

Lacy nodded her agreement. "And I'll be keepin' a sharp eye out on Helena. If that little girl gets ta bein' happy agin anytime soon, we'll have the pair of 'em to be watchin', don't ye know."

The Duke of Glynde had always thought himself to be a sane man, a rational man, a fair man. He was good to his tenant farmers and servant staff, a loving son to his late parents, a mentor to his brother, and a loyal friend. He generously supported his church, dutifully took up his seat in Parliament every January, and had never bedded another man's wife. He was, he had always believed, a gentleman.

So why did he feel he was such a monster, one of the lowest of the low? Why did he stomp about the house wearing a scowl that sent the maids to scurrying for the kitchens? Why had he been spending so much of his time away from home, gaming and drinking and generally avoiding all contact with the gaggle of women that had taken up residence in Portman Square?

Most important, why had he found it impossible to meet Beatrice Stourbridge's eyes whenever he was forced into her company? Was he embarrassed? Was he ashamed? Was he confused? Was he hurt?

Yes, dammit, he thought as he strode up St. James's just past noon, he was all of those things—and more. He was embarrassed and ashamed that he had been so blockheaded as to believe that Trixy had cared for him more than she cared for her own comfort. She may have admitted to wanting him, but she had been just as quick to grab at the cottage and allowance once more while admitting that she would pass it all over in a moment if she thought there was a deeper gravy boat—such as Sir Roderick and the possibility of a more permanent arrangement in the form of marriage—anywhere near that she could jump into with both feet.

Harry was also confused, for even now, a week later, he was having trouble sorting out all that had happened that fateful night of the twins' come-out ball. Trixy's calmly uttered protestations of business being business might still peal in his ears, but he couldn't completely banish the niggling thought that she had been genuinely caught off-guard by his bald offer to set her up as his mistress.

His hands clenched into fists. No! He was not going to allow himself to think that way. He was not going to allow the memory of those soulful green eyes and that single, probably purposely produced tear to trick him into believing, not for the first time, that Trixy was an innocent. No innocent young lady, no matter how hard-pressed she might be by circumstances, ever holds a gun, figuratively or literally, to a man's head and demands satisfaction in the way of money and a place to live. Not in Harry's memory, anyway.

He had been right to limit his involvement with her to that of man and mistress. He had no plans to marry at the moment, and when he did decide to enter that condition, it most certainly would not be with a woman who had threatened to expose his brother as a kidnapper and ruin both William's and his good name. That was ludicrous!

So as he walked up St. James's, the Duke of Glynde acknowledged that he was embarrassed, ashamed, and confused. He could live with all those feelings if he had to, he supposed, for the Season would be over before he knew it and Trixy and the Somerville twins would be out of his life forever.

But he was also hurt, and hurt deeply, for he recognized at last that his heart was involved. And that particular hurt, he knew, wouldn't pass out of his life quite so easily.

"What, ho! Harry! Wait up, will you? I've been chasing you for nearly a half-mile, trying to catch you up. I would have yelled to you, but I'm older now and have learned to be more circumspect. Where are you off to in such a rush, anyway?"

Harry, who had been running away from himself rather than heading toward any one place, stopped to see Sir Roderick Hilliard bearing down on him from behind. "Another new pair of Hessians, Roddy? You really ought to strive more for comfort in your rig-outs than for style. You're not walking —you're mincing. Besides, the pain makes you frown. All in all, I'd say you're not a pretty sight."

Sir Roderick, rather breathless from his exertion, stopped beside his friend to look at him owlishly. "You're being rather cutting today, aren't you, Harry? What's the matter? You've been acting queer as Dick's hatband ever since we got back to town. It can't be that you're still worried about how society feels about your bringing out Myles's offspring, for everyone thinks you're a saint for taking care of the girls after their rotter of a father abandoned them. Besides, it ain't as if the lines are bad or they smell of the shop. It's only Myles that turned bad."

Harry, who was well aware that his guardianship of the Somerville twins had somehow nominated him for sainthood—an occurrence more easily understood when his extreme wealth and considerable consequence were taken into account—merely smiled and began walking once more.

"Where are we going, Harry?" Sir Roderick asked, keeping pace with the duke's long strides only through some personal sacrifice, since his new boots were pinching abominably. "It's too early to be out gaming, as if you haven't been playing deep all week long—when you aren't sitting by yourself in some corner sulking, that is. You remind me of Salty. When he's not with Miss Eugenie, he's sulking. He's beginning to get on my nerves too, now that I think of it."

Sir Roderick stopped in his tracks, grabbing at Harry's arm. "Could that be it, Harry? Are you in love as well? That would make three of us, you know. Dropping like flies, aren't we? Must be something in the air. Who is it?"

The duke, who had been racking his brain for some way of escaping his loquacious acquaintance, looked at Sir Roderick blankly. "Who is what, Roddy? What are you talking about?"

"Why, your ladylove, of course," Sir Roderick answered, tipping his hat to two gentlemen approaching from the opposite direction, and then craning his neck to watch them pass by them down the flagway. "Did you see Freddie's coat, Harry? What shade of ugly was it, do you think? I've always wondered if Freddie was blind to color—you know, not seeing things for what they are. It certainly would explain that coat, wouldn't it, even if it wouldn't explain his horse-faced wife. Now, what was the question? Oh, yes, I remember now. Salty's in love with Miss Eugenie, I'm in love with my darling Trixy—whom are you in love with, Harry?"

"You . . . you're in love with Trixy . . . with Miss Stourbridge?"

Sir Roderick laughed aloud. "Well, stap me, of course I am, Harry. Why else do you think I've been perched on your doorstep all week? Whom did you think I was in love with—your aunt? Salty would have my guts for garters if I looked at his Eugenie sideways. And I'm certainly not in love with that doomsday-faced Miss Helena Somerville. You know, for twins, it's easy enough to tell them apart. Does she ever smile, Harry?"

"You're really in love with Trixy?" Harry seemed to be having some difficulty assimilating this one single fact. "Truly?"

Sir Roderick stopped dead in order to make a show of crossing his heart. "Truly, Harry. Oh, I know you're surprised, as well you should be, for I've never really been much in the petticoat line, but Trixy isn't quite your ordinary miss, you know."

"Yes," Harry answered carefully, "I have become almost painfully aware of that fact. But do you really think you have been in her company long enough to be certain of your feelings? I mean, there may be facets of her character—that is, of her personality—that you wouldn't like."

Sir Roderick's grin faded, to be replaced by a scowl. "I say, Harry, that's not nice. What do you have against Trixy, anyway? It isn't like you to . . . Oh! I get it now. You don't want me to be in love with Trixy because you are yourself! Of course! I should have seen it sooner. My God, Harry—we're rivals! I'm not quite sure that I like that."

"We are not rivals, Roddy, and I'm not in love with Miss Stourbridge. Sometimes you make less sense than William or his half-witted friend, Andrew." Harry waved to a passing hackney coach, flagging it down with the intention of climbing into it and getting himself as far away from Sir Roderick and his questions as was humanly possible.

Sir Roderick was nothing if not persistent. "Well, then, Harry, if you want me to believe you—tell me whom you *are* in love with, if you can."

"Why do I have to be in love with anyone?" Harry

countered when Sir Roderick seemed determined to get some sort of answer out of him before allowing him to enter the hackney cab.

"Because you're acting as queer as Dick's hatband. I already told you that," Sir Roderick persisted, ignoring the hackney driver's admonition to the gentlemen to either climb aboard or shove off, but to do it quickly, as he had five mouths to feed at home and needed as many fares as he could get before his nag died of old age waiting for gentry morts to make up their minds whether or not they wanted to go anywhere.

Harry turned to his friend. "I'm sorry my disposition bothers you, Roddy, but I promise you I am not in love. Perhaps my liver is just slightly off or something. Now, please, I must be on my way. Mention of my brother and his friend has reminded me that I heard the two of them mumbling something this morning at breakfast about a cockfight taking place somewhere. I want to make sure they didn't bet over their heads and end up stuffed into the basket over the arena or some such thing."

At last Harry was safely in the hackney cab, and safely alone, since Sir Roderick had sworn long ago—after ruining one of his best jackets by sitting on something unrecognizable but decidedly vile while riding in one—that he would never set foot, or rump, in one of the contraptions again.

"Deny it all you want, old man, I still say you're in love with someone," Harry could hear Sir Roderick call after him as the cab pulled out into the light early-afternoon traffic. He slunk down on the greasy leather seat, determined to spend the remainder of the day and evening finding himself another, less discerning set of friends.

15

ANDREW CARLISLE wandered aimlessly into the morning room, his long, pointed chin nearly dragging on the carpet. London should have been more fun than it had proved thus far, he was sure of it, but even the thought of a rousing cockfight hadn't been enough to budge Willie from the house that day. Nothing, not even a trip to Astley's or one of the infamous inns in Tothill Fields or even a chance at sneaking into a gaming hell seemed to be enough to propel Willie more than a pebble's toss from the place, as a matter of fact.

It was damned depressing, that's what it was, to see his best friend moping around from morn till night hoping for a smile from the fair Helena, who had been smiling even less than Willie had been, now that Andy considered the thing.

As a matter of fact, there didn't appear to be anybody doing a precious lot of giggling in Portman Square these days, except maybe for Lady Amelia, who seemed to be having the time of her life presenting the twins, or that jaw-me-dead Sir

Roderick Hilliard, who fancied himself in love with Beatrice Stourbridge and could talk a three-days-dead corpse into picking up his coffin and toddling away. Andy wondered how in love Sir Roderick would stay if he ever turned around one fine night to see Trixy pointing a pistol at him.

So lost in his brown study was Andy that it took him a few minutes to realize that he wasn't alone in the morning room, that a chair in the far corner was occupied by a weeping Somerville twin—which one, he could never be sure, for they were as alike as two peas in a pod.

Willie would have known, for Willie had vowed a thousand times that Helena, who had a single burnt-cinnamon fleck in her left eye, was by far the prettier of the two. Andy, who couldn't have cared less for flecks—cinnamon or otherwise—or for females in general, for that matter, saw the Somerville twins only as blond, annoyingly prone to tears, and totally unnecessary to his happiness.

He looked about the room for a moment, deciding whether it would be safer—if rather cowardly—to leave before the chit spied him out, but as her weeping turned to rather loud, nerve-shredding sobs, he manfully approached her chair and asked if there might be anything in particular he could do to be of assistance.

He sincerely hoped she would simply thank him for his offer but say no, for she might just take it into her head to ask to borrow his handkerchief, and if there was one thing Andy was sure of, it was that if he lent the thing for her to use, he most certainly didn't then want her to hand it back to him.

A moment later his worst fears were realized, and he reached into his pocket and reluctantly passed over the handkerchief before turning to beat a hasty retreat before she could return it.

"You're so kind and thoughtful, Andy, even if your face looks as if you should be preaching dusty sermons and telling everyone it's a terrible sin to have fun," Miss Somerville said on a sob, halting him in his tracks with the unconscious insult. "I shouldn't be in here, I know, where just anyone could walk in on me and see me at my worst, but Eugenie is closeted upstairs with Lacy, doing something with her hair—I think she plans to wear it in the Grecian style tonight—and I had nowhere else to go."

Andy gave a single nod of his head. All right, so now he knew that the watering pot was Helena, Willie's object of passion. He had also learned a lot of things he didn't much care to know about, but that was the way women talked, he knew, always saying tons more than any man of sense needed to hear.

"What are you bawling about, anyway, Helena?" he asked baldly, finesse never being his forte. "Don't tell me you're mooning over Willie, for it won't fadge. He'd have you in a minute, and well you know it."

"Willie?" Helena blew her nose prodigiously, then looked up at Andy in confusion. "Willie has developed a *tendre* for me?" Her gaze slid away from his. "Oh, isn't that kind? He is adorable, isn't he, Andy? I like him ever so much, and he is very pretty, as I told the duke, so much so that I did believe for a moment, no more, that I might care for him, but . . ." Her voice broke on yet another, to Andy, annoying sob. "But my heart . . . my heart is pledged to another!"

Andy plopped himself down in a nearby chair, his long, bird-thin legs jutting out in front of him. "Well, if that don't beat the Dutch! Here I am in London, ready to kick up a lark or two, and all I'm doing is kicking my heels around here, watching Willie go all arsy-varsy over a chit who thinks he's pretty—but is crying buckets over someone else!"

He made to rise. "Excuse me, won't you? I want to go run Willie to ground and give him the good news. Maybe there's still time to catch the cockfight. Oh, by the by, you can keep my handkerchief. I don't really think I want it anymore."

He had taken no more than three steps before Helena's sobs stopped him in his tracks. Obviously she hadn't liked that bit about the handkerchief. "Oh, good grief!" he exclaimed, his mama's lessons about damsels in distress and all that terrible garbage he'd had to listen to when his cousin Lizzie had visited last summer forcing him to turn around and offer his gentlemanly assistance yet a second time.

"What's his name," he muttered resignedly, seating himself once more, "and what do I have to do to make you turn off the waterworks?"

Trixy heard Harry before she saw him, his angry, raised voice meeting her halfway through the foyer on her way to the drawing room. "One hundred and forty pounds for gloves? For gloves? Last time I looked, Aunt Amelia, the girls each had only two hands. What are these gloves made of—unicorn hide? . . . No, you say? Well, it must be something equally rare to cost one hundred and forty pounds."

Trixy entered the drawing room to see Harry, dressed in his evening clothes, pacing agitatedly in front of the settee, both his hands full of trades-men's bills, while a stylishly clad Lady Amelia perched nervously on the very edge of the settee like a child called before its parent for a scolding, her hands twisting in her lap.

"We could not stint, you know, nephew," Lady Amelia said, her head moving from side to side as she followed the duke's path up and down the carpet. "With the piddling portions you settled on dear Eugenie and Helena to lure husbands for them, it was imperative we outfit them to their best advantage. A pretty frame for a pretty picture, we always say."

Harry stopped to turn about abruptly and wave a sheaf of bills at the woman. "And what do 'we say' about this bill for a single sea-green gown, madam, if everything was for the twins, whom you've been dressing alike from head to foot? That's what I really want to know. And this bill—for a single jonquil gown, and a single Clarence-blue walking dress, and a single bottle-green pelisse with swansdown trim—must I go on?"

Trixy, who was standing just behind him, wearing the "single jonquil gown," bit her lip and waited for Lady Amelia to explain. "Why, don't be silly, nephew," the woman began, giggling, "you know those things were for your dearest Trixy—"

"My dearest Trixy?" Harry interrupted, his angry

bellow threatening to straighten the tight gray curls in Lady Amelia's hair. "Then it is just as I thought when I came home today to find my study knee-deep in bills! The woman's a companion to the twins, Aunt, and a necessary evil, but she's not my 'dearest' anything! Whatever gave you such a hare-brained idea?"

"But . . . but you said . . . or at least we thought you said . . . but maybe, now that we think on it, perhaps it was dearest Trixy who said . . . Oh, dear, we're so confused!"

"Good evening, all," Trixy hastened to interrupt just as she was sure Lady Amelia was going to give the game away by remembering that it had been Trixy who had told her the duke wanted the twin's companion rigged out for the Season, although she had been following his orders—sort of. "My goodness, Lady Amelia, don't you look especially lovely this evening? And you, Harry. Are you by chance joining us at Lady Hereford's? Roddy will like that, as he was just saying last night that he doesn't see enough of you anymore."

"I saw enough of him this afternoon to last him for a while, I should think." Glynde whirled about to face Trixy, his hot gaze running quickly up and down the length of her, then switching to the jumble of bills he held in his hands.

"Jonquil, I presume, Miss Stourbridge?" he said at last, smiling evilly. "How gratifying it is for me to help you bait your hook for Sir Roderick. You don't do anything by half-measures, do you?" He bowed in her direction. "My compliments, madam. You do your 'business'—and your entire profession —proud."

Trixy dropped him a quick curtsy. "Thank you, your grace," she said evenly, knowing the worst was past—for, indeed, nothing could be worse than the opinion the duke already had of her. "One does what one can to keep body and soul together in these trying times."

"We don't think we understand," Lady Amelia piped up, her voice very small. "Didn't you want us to outfit Trixy? We could hardly have her accompanying the girls in anything taken from the meager wardrobe she had with her at Glyndevaron. Besides, nephew, as we have been assured you are interested in Trixy for yourself, we certainly couldn't see you allowing her to be embarrassed in any way. Oh, dear. Poor Harry—has Sir Roderick beaten you out? No wonder you're so crotchety. We're prodigiously sorry."

At Lady Amelia's last words, Harry looked piercingly at Trixy and mouthed something that she was sure was "I'll get you for this" before turning back to his aunt. "Forgive me, Aunt Amelia—I've been acting the fool. Of course I wanted you to outfit Trixy as well as the twins. And I do hope there are purchases for yourself numbered among these bills. I was just overset—not having ever launched anyone before—and was momentarily taken aback by the cost of the thing. Two dozen pairs of gloves? Now that I think on it—are you quite sure two dozen pairs are enough?"

"Thank you, nephew. And Sir Roderick?" his aunt pursued, beginning to look teary-eyed.

"Ah, dearest aunt," Harry countered with a wink that could have meant anything, "who is to say about matters of the heart? Will the girls be down soon? It's growing late, and you know how Lady Hereford is about punctuality."

Trixy hid a smile behind her hand as Harry threatened to make a cake of himself trying to redirect his aunt—who had immediately risen to ring Pinch to check on the twins—but her smile faded quickly when she perceived he would deal less kindly with his "dearest Trixy" sometime later, when he found her alone.

Willie and Andy entered the drawing room close behind Pinch, relieving Trixy from the trouble of attempting to stay clear of Harry and his bound-to-be-cutting whispers until the twins came downstairs and they could leave for Lady Hereford's.

"And I still say she is not," Willie was protesting hotly as the two walked to the drinks table, barely nodding to the other occupants of the drawing room.

"She is too," Andy answered, pouring himself a glass of sherry, which was all Harry would allow either of the boys to drink. "Not only that, but she's most probably not going with us tonight, so sick with love the chit is. I tell you, Willie, you're wasting your time. Better to skip this dull hash tonight and buy a ticket for the stalls. If we're lucky, the play will be bad and we can toss cabbages at the stage."

"Not going?" Willie halted in the midst of pouring himself a glass of sherry. "You never mean it, Andy. And me spending above an hour trying to get this neckcloth right. How ungrateful can a woman be? Why, you know what, Andy, I believe I'm getting heartily sick of this love business. I never bathed half so much, for one thing—and I don't think I even like to dance."

"Then we can go to the theater?"

Willie slammed down the glass so hard that a bit of sherry splashed onto his shirt cuff, but he didn't take any notice. "To the theater, and to Astley's tomorrow, and to a mill if we can find one where the fighters are promised to go at least twenty rounds! Now, come on, Andy, there's no sense hanging around here all night, is there?"

Trixy, Harry, and Lady Amelia watched in silence as the two boys walked arm in arm out of the room without acknowledging anyone else's presence.

"We sometimes wonder about our nephew," Lady Amelia said slowly after the front door slammed shut behind the boys a few moments later. "We think he takes a bit too much after our dear, departed Uncle Augustus. You remember, nephew, Uncle Augustus was the one we visited in Herefordshire. Never married, and was all the time taking off his boots in company to talk to his toes."

Harry caught Trixy's eye and, in a rare moment of complete harmony, the two openly smiled at each other as one of the twins floated into the room, looking exquisite, although sad, in her white taffeta gown.

"Eugenie has the headache, Lady Amelia, and has taken to her bed," she said, looking down at her toes, her entire body displaying the attitude of melancholy the girl had donned like a cloak around the time of the come-out ball and had refused to discard ever since. "She has Lacy with her, and has begged us to go on without her."

"Oh, dear," Lady Amelia said worriedly, her hands once more twisting in her lap. "We like it so much better when both of them are together—they match so perfectly, you understand, that they attract the most wonderful compliments, for which we may take at least some of the credit, as we had the outfitting of them. And Mr. Saltaire will be terribly upset when we meet him at Lady Hereford's and he learns that his Eugenie has taken to her bed."

She turned to Trixy, who was busily inspecting Helena as if for flaws, a confused frown on her face. "Perhaps you might forgo the evening's entertainment, my dear, to bear our poor little Eugenie company in her discomfort."

"She will not," Harry answered before Trixy could open her mouth, for he had decided that he was not about to stand back idly while his good friend Sir Roderick literally threw his life away on such a calculated, conniving hussy, and he had a few plans of his own for the evening. "Her maid is with her, and that should be sufficient."

Trixy broke off her scrutiny of Helena to look at Harry out of the corners of her eyes, sensing that the duke had something nasty up his sleeve but not knowing exactly what it was.

"Eugenie is probably still worried about Mr. Saltaire's toplofty mother opposing a match between them," she offered by way of explanation. "Her maid told me all about it. Poor, dear Eugenie."

Helena emitted a small sob, causing Lady Amelia to ask if both twins might be sickening for something, but Harry stepped in quickly to repeat his admonishment about Lady Hereford's dislike of tardiness, and within five minutes the party was on its way outside to the waiting coach.

Upstairs, peeking out from behind the draperies in her bedchamber, the supposedly ailing Miss Somerville—who still had the fingers of one hand crossed behind her back—grinned from ear to ear for the first time in a long while.

16

TRIXY YANKED at the intricate clasp of the garnet necklace, nearly breaking it in her haste to rid herself of any reminder of the gathering at Lady Hereford's. It had been quite the most frustrating, unhappy, and maddening few hours of her life, and she had the horrid, insufferable, obnoxious Duke of Glynde to thank for every miserable moment of it!

From the moment Sir Roderick had entered the Hereford drawing room to take up his place beside Trixy, Harry had not budged from her other side, his contributions to the conversation dealing with tales of fortune-hunting females and their hapless victims, various forms of torture employed by nobles in the Middle Ages on thieves and blackmailers who dared ply their trades on them, the prospects of any gently bred female prisoner reaching Australia without perishing along the way, and innumerable other subjects too terrible in content to contemplate.

Sir Roderick, whom Trixy had grown to like very

much, but who seemed to reckon himself an expert on everything and, likewise, appeared unafraid to expound on that "everything" without a thought to the notion that he might be boring his audience to flinders, had joined into each discussion at some length, not realizing that Trixy, who knew exactly what Harry was trying to do, had believed herself to be dying a slow, agonizing death for the entirety of the evening.

Tying the sash of her dressing gown about her waist, Trixy sat at her dressing table to begin taking the pins from her hair. How she longed for the Season to be over so that she could leave London and do her best to forget she had ever clapped eyes on the Duke of Glynde. Her fingers halting in midair, she stared at her reflection in the mirror, to discover that she was crying.

How could she be such an idiot as to love any man that much? "Oh, Harry," she said on a sigh, "I do love you—even if you believe me to be a heartless, fortune-hunting blackmailer."

"Trixy?"

She turned about quickly, a hand going to the neckline of her dressing gown. "You!" she exclaimed in disbelief as she saw the duke's head poking around the open door to her chamber. "What do you want? It must be past three in the morning—and I'm not dressed. Have you taken leave of your senses, or have you come to gloat over your ridiculous behavior tonight?"

"Keep your voice down, for pity's sake, or else you'll have my aunt in here declaring I've compromised you and demanding we wed at once." Glynde walked into the room, a sheet of paper in his hand.

Trixy wiped surreptitiously at her tears and rose. "Your point is well-taken. We wouldn't want anything so terrible to happen, would we, Harry? Yet, now that I think on it, if the hints you were dropping all night to Sir Roderick finally serve to bring to his attention my most grievous faults, perhaps I might consider saving myself by considering such a scheme. You already know that I am beyond nothing when it comes to securing my own comfort."

Harry wasn't listening, at least not very carefully. He was too intent on his reason for coming to see her at this hour of the morning. "Stop thinking only of yourself a moment, Trixy," he admonished meanly, causing her head to snap back as if she had been slapped. "I stumbled over this note in my study. I don't think I was supposed to see it until tomorrow morning, but women being as scatter-brained as they are, who's to know?" He thrust the paper into her nerveless hands. "Here. See if you can make head or tail of it."

Trixy walked over to the nearby brace of candles and applied herself to reading the childish scrawl. "Oh, my Lord, Helena's gone!" she exclaimed when she was done. "I should have known it! No wonder Helena was so in the doldrums all night, watching Mr. Saltaire from across the room as he performed his duty dances. It wasn't Helena at Lady Hereford's at all—it was Eugenie! It all makes sense to me now."

"What are you talking about?" Harry asked, sprawling in a chair. "That note says Helena has run off with some blackguard named Percy, which is impossible, because Helena has been with us all evening long. I found the note before she could put her plan into motion, which is why I came to you. You'll have to talk some sense into her head."

He sat up very straight, as the whole of what Trixy had said penetrated his weary brain. "Are you telling me that it wasn't Helena who was with us, but Eugenie—with the real Helena staying home with the headache, pretending she was Eugenie? My God!" He hopped to his feet. "Quickly, woman. Go to their rooms and count noses!"

Trixy put a hand to her mouth. "I will if you insist, but I doubt that it will do more than prove me right. I had a feeling there was something strange about Helena—Eugenie, that is—this evening, but I couldn't put my finger on it. I usually don't have much trouble telling them apart, unless they don't want me to know which is which. Obviously tonight was one of those times."

She sat herself down on the edge of the bed, shaking her head. "What a sad hash I've made of everything, Harry. If I hadn't been so concerned over whatever mischief you had planned for tonight, I should have seen through their deception in a moment. Now Helena has run off to Gretna Green with Percival Sauveur." She shook her head, shaking off some of her guilt. "This is all your fault, you know, Harry, now that I think on it."

"My fault? My fault!" Harry crossed the room in a half-dozen quick strides, to place himself squarely in front of Trixy. "Oh, you're a real piece of work, aren't you, Miss Stourbridge? I put a roof over your head, clothes on your back, watch as you lead my friend on a merry dance—and now it's my fault that the one thing you were supposed to do in order to earn your keep, running herd on the twins, has ended in a shambles. I warn you, madam, I am feeling an almost overwhelming urge to break open your head, just so that I might see how that twisted brain of yours works!"

He whirled away, to begin pacing the carpet, before turning back to her. "And just who or what in bloody hell is Percival Sauveur?"

Trixy's shoulders lifted and fell in a great sigh. "He's the French dancing master hired to tutor the twins when first we came to London. The dancing master that you hired, Harry, if you'll recall."

The duke slapped a palm hard against his forehead. "Oh, that's above everything wonderful! A dancing master. And now you're twisting it around so that you can lay more blame at my feet—because I'm the one who chose him? Go ahead, feel free, madam. I'm a grown man—I can take it."

"Oh, stifle yourself." Trixy had had enough. "Monsieur Sauveur is a very nice young man, the son of some aristocrat who fled here during the Terror and never went back. Monsieur Sauveur might be poor, but he is from a good family. If you give me a moment, I may be able to remember his title. It's very long and involved, as I recall."

"And that makes everything right, I suppose? God, to be a woman, and have a woman's sense of logic!" Glynde stomped back to where Trixy was sitting and pulled her to her feet. "How do you suppose Eugenie will be allowed to wed her Salty now—once his mother catches wind of Helena's flight? Not only have you damned me, madam, to supporting Helena and her tippy-toed frog throughout eternity, but I shall never be rid of Eugenie either, unless Salty decides to marry over the anvil as well. I'm chin-deep in expensive, glove-buying women, Miss Stourbridge, and I don't like it! I don't bloody well like it at all!"

Trixy threw back her head and glared up into his face. "Why, you poor oppressed man," she declared vehemently. "Far be it from me to point out that this entire business started when your brother took it into his maggot-infested head to serve up Eugenie and Helena in your bed like sacrificial virgins so that you could revenge yourself on their father. Far be it from me to point out that, after volunteering to sponsor the twins for the Season, you have done nothing but roar around here like a lion with a sore paw, moaning about modiste bills that any nursery toddler could have told you are part and parcel of launching a young miss. Far be it from me to—"

"Shut up!" Harry commanded, remembering what had happened the last time Trixy dared to gift him with a cataloging of his sins. He wasn't about to fall into that trap again—kissing her to cut off her damning truths. If he kissed her again, he might never be able to let her go, no matter how larcenous her nature. Still, the idea did have some appeal, and he made no move to put some sanity-restoring space between them.

Trixy, who had also remembered the end result of their last argument, bit her lip and lowered her head. "I'm sorry, Harry. We're both overset about

Helena, I suppose. Don't you think we should be rousing the household and setting off after her? She can't have gotten very far."

Harry liked the feel of soft silk beneath his hands and began running his fingers lightly up and down Trixy's slim arms. "It has begun raining buckets out there," he heard himself say, amazed at his sudden lack of interest in Helena Somerville. "It would be a messy ride, and we can't be sure which road they took, or if they're riding in a stagecoach."

"That's true enough," Trixy agreed quietly, a small fire starting somewhere in her stomach as she was once more brought to the realization of where they were and how she was dressed—or undressed. "And she just might run away again after we've gone to all the trouble of fetching her home. She was terribly unhappy, poor darling, and now we know it was for love of her Percy. Yes, she'd probably just run off again. Helena can be very determined. We would have put ourselves out for nothing."

Harry nodded, noticing not for the first time that Trixy's jasmine-scented perfume suited her perfectly. Go haring out after Helena? Why would he want to do such a thing when it was so warm and cozy here, in Trixy's bedchamber? "Eugenie seems to have given her blessing to the match, or else she wouldn't have helped her make good her escape. She's the child's only family—as I don't count deserting papas as family. Who are we to object if Helena's sister is agreeable to the marriage?"

"You'll still turn over the portion you set aside

for her?" Trixy asked, deliberately staring at his cravat, as his tone had turned low and seductive, even if his words were anything but loverlike.

He nodded. "And even pay her an allowance as long as she promises to stay at least one hundred miles from any of my houses," he added, chuckling. "So, I guess that's all settled then, isn't it? This launching business isn't so bad after all. One down, one to go."

Trixy kept her eyes averted. "I think I've found a way around Mrs. Saltaire's objections," she told him, wishing her breathing could be more regular. "The woman is very involved in charity work. Eugenie is also very interested in doing good deeds. I think if we could just get the two of them together and set them to talking to each other—"

"We'd have Salty and Eugenie neatly bracketed before the king's birthday!" Harry concluded happily, as all the little puzzle pieces began to fall so neatly into place. He sobered suddenly and took his hands from Trixy's shoulders, allowing them to glide slowly downward to grasp her slim waist. "And then what, Trixy, hmm? Would you still want that cottage by the sea—or do your plans also run to matrimony?"

She tried to move away from Harry's grasp, but the bed was directly behind her and she had nowhere to go. "What do you think, Harry?" she asked breathlessly, daring to look up at him.

"Roddy believes himself madly in love with you. He'd talk you straight into an early grave, but he is sincere. I think he'd marry you even if I told him the truth about you."

Her gaze searched his, her heart on fire with the love she was sure he'd throw back into her face if she dared to declare it. "And what is the truth about me, Harry? Do you know? Do you even care?"

He lifted a hand to stroke the side of her face, then pushed his fingers into her unbound hair. "I thought I did. I think I do—and then again, I'm not sure. Sometimes I think you want me to believe the worst of you, Trixy. But then, there are other times, times when I watch you being so kind to my aunt, times when I overhear you drilling the girls on their manners or laughing and teasing Willie and Andy the way you never have me . . ." He took a deep breath. "Those are the times that I believe I did you a grave injustice in asking you to become my mistress."

This was wrong. This was all so very, very wrong. Alone together in her chamber, with his defenses down, Trixy knew she was within an inch of having Harry declare for her. His eyes were burning so brightly that Trixy felt as if she would burst into flame if she didn't find some way of deflecting the heat that threatened to consume them both.

Only in the morning, when he had more time to think, would he realize that he had let the passion of the moment overcome his deep-down conviction that she was a scheming blackmailer, and then he would hate her even more.

She wanted nothing more than to have him believe she was innocent, to make him see that circumstances, and not inclination, had led her to the point where she had demanded payment for her silence about his brother's rash maneuver, but deep in her heart she knew that she had indeed succumbed to the temptation to improve her own lot while she was at it. She had concocted that whole stupid blackmail scheme, and she had, at least for a time, entertained every notion of carrying out that scheme to the letter.

She was a soiled woman, a criminal, no matter how noble her intentions—and how noble could they have been, considering that she had not been satisfied with gaining rescue for the twins, but had gone on recklessly demanding that her own nest be feathered as well?

Still, Harry was standing so close to her. His lips were within scant inches of hers, his hard body only a whisper away. She wouldn't inflict herself on him, or take what he offered, only to see his love turn to scorn as he remembered how she had tried to manipulate his life. But couldn't she have one last kiss, one last memory to cling to, before she did the noble thing and walked out of his life?

"Harry, I . . ." she began, raising her hands to his chest, to bury them in the intricate folds of his snowy white cravat.

"Trixy, my darling . . ." he returned huskily, his head bending to hers.

"And isn't this a pretty sight, and no mistake. Playing at slap and tickle with his worship, is it? A body would think the money would be enough fer ye. Would ye be wantin' by chance ta know what's been goin' on whilst ye two been doin' whatever it is ye're doin' in here? My Helena's up and gone off ta wed that Frenchie prancin' master, that's what."

"Lacy!" Trixy exclaimed, nearly toppling onto the

bed as the duke turned, shielding her with his body. "This . . . this isn't what you think," she said, peeking around Harry's shoulder and cudgeling her brain for some explanation that would save the duke from disgrace. "His grace has been . . . has been comforting me, as he found the note Helena left when she eloped with Monsieur Sauveur, and I . . . I felt faint when I heard the news."

The maid merely sniffed, saying something about tugging at her other leg, as it had bells on it, and launched into a recitation of her own problems. "Dosed me good with some of me own laudanum, that tricky little colleen did, so that I just woke up, don't ye know. I roused Eugenie with a cuff on the ear—I was that mad—and she told me the whole of it.

"Blessed Mother and all the saints, but I never expected this. Never met a pretty girl yet what had the sense of a newborn babe when it came ta men. Helena's already as good as lost ta us, I suppose— although it's my guess she'll be sniffing back here once the deed is done—but now that there's only one chick ta watch, no more foxes will be gettin' past me inta the henhouse, if ye take m'meanin'."

She made to leave the room, holding her head and complaining of having "the divil of a headache," before turning back to glare at Trixy. "Just a word o' warnin', missy, though why I'm botherin', I can't tell ye. He won't be marryin' ye, ye know. As me sainted mother used to say, they never does wed the cow when they can gets the milk fer free."

Trixy collapsed onto the edge of the bed the moment the door closed behind the maid, hiding her face in her hands. Harry quickly sat down beside her, putting a comforting arm around her shoulders, which had begun to shake visibly. "I'm so sorry, darling," he crooned into her hair. "I'll go after the woman, and make her understand. Please . . . don't cry."

"Cry?" Trixy exclaimed, raising her head so that the duke could see the tears streaming down her cheeks even as she grinned at him. "Why would I cry?" she asked, doubling over again in laughter.

"Trixy . . . ?" he asked, confused.

She took a deep breath, trying to regain control of herself. "That has to be the funniest thing I've ever seen. Did you get a good look at her, Harry? Her nightgown would make a tolerable sail for a man-o'-war, and her nightcap hanging over her eyes made her look like a drunken sailor out on a spree. And you—you standing in front of me as if you were saving my reputation, the reputation you don't believe in, while you had only moments earlier been trying to do just what Lacy said you were trying to do. What a mad farce we all are! Oh, Lord, my sides ache!"

Harry, his amorous pursuit stymied—and his interest effectively quashed by the maid's statement of what had, he admitted silently, been his intentions—took refuge in anger. Rising from the bed, he glowered down at Trixy, who was now lying back on the bed, her arms wrapped around her waist as she gave in once more to mirth.

"I fail to see the humor," he declared coldly, although, in truth, the corners of his lips had begun to twitch. "If anything, I should say we've both had a happy escape. Good night to you, madam!" With that, and with Trixy's uninhibited giggles urging him on his way, he left her chamber to make for his study once more, and the bottle that awaited him there.

17

THE DUKE OF GLYNDE had only limited memories of his mother, because she had succumbed to childbed fever eighteen years ago, when William was born, but he instinctively knew that she was perhaps the one woman in the world who might be able to help him now. His mother, he was sure, would know how to handle Trixy, how to look her deep in the eyes and figure out what the dratted girl was thinking.

"And, maybe, just maybe, Mother would be able to pinpoint exactly where I went wrong," Harry told the nearly empty brandy glass he was staring into at that moment, the same glass he had been filling and refilling all night, until the rain had stopped and the late-morning sun had at last begun filtering through the curtains into his study.

It had been a long night, the empty hours haunted by the memory of Trixy's tear-edged laughter as he had all but slunk out of her bedchamber to creep back down the steps to his study, and he was still dressed in his evening clothes, although they were, at the moment, very much the worse for wear, not that Willie seemed to notice that fact as he careered into the room without bothering to knock.

"Harry! There you are! Good!" Willie exclaimed in full throat as he immediately took up pacing the carpet, his hands clenched into fists. "You'll never believe it, Harry! Helena's run off—and it's all Andy's doing, the coldhearted blackguard! He told me the whole of it this morning, as if it were some tremendous joke. He arranged for the coach and driver—and even gave them some of his own blunt, as if he ever had two coppers to rub together this close to the end of the quarter. How could he have done this to me, to his best friend? I popped him one, o'course—right in the dining room—and now I demand satisfaction."

Harry lifted his bloodshot gaze to his brother, noticing yet again how terribly, terribly young the lad was. "You demand satisfaction for popping him one?" he asked, raising one eyebrow. "I think you have that the wrong way around, William—unless you wish for Andy to pop you one back? Do you think that's wise? I mean, you should try to remember that your nose has an unfortunate propensity for bleeding."

"What?" Willie whirled about to face his brother, his eyes wild as he ran a hand through his already disheveled hair. "Don't laugh at me, Harry. This ain't funny! This ain't funny in the least!"

Harry begged to differ, as he was finding the scene unfolding in front of him to be laughable in the extreme—which probably just went to show how excessively put upon he was feeling at that moment—but he wisely didn't put thought into speech. Instead, he calmly pointed out that just last night Lord William had declared in front of one and all that he was no longer in love with the fair Helena.

"That is nothing to the point, Harry!" Willie countered, dropping abjectly to his knees in front of his brother, all the better to plead his case. "Don't you see? My best friend—my bosom chum—has betrayed me! I am devastated!"

Harry frowned, as if considering this argument. "Helena ran off with her dancing master, after mooning about the house over the man for the past several weeks—not that we knew it at the time. Personally, I had just believed her gloves to be too tight. Be that as it may, this eloping business doesn't seem to be the action of a rational woman, William. I'd say, upon reflection, that you've had a most fortunate escape. As a matter of fact, you might just owe Andy an apology—unless you plan on mounting your trusty steed and riding off after the chit before she can be completely ruined?"

Willie sat back on his haunches, his nose screwed up as he considered this last question. "Ride off after her? Now, why do you suppose I should want to do a crackbrained thing like that, Harry? It ain't like she's family or anything, and she did leave us of her own free will. Besides, there's going to be a splendid mill just outside Wimbledon today, and I've already promised Andy we would go."

He hopped to his feet. "Andy! My God, Harry—when I left him he was dipping his serviette into the water pitcher and putting it to his eye. I could have blinded the fellow! Excuse me—I must go check on him at once. Really, Harry, I think you could have pointed that out to me. I thought you liked Andy."

"And I thought you were going to call him out, William," Harry quickly reminded the youth, doing his best to hide his amusement. "That is why you came storming in here, isn't it?"

Willie looked askance over his shoulder at his brother. "Call him out? Who? Andy? My best friend —the man what may have saved me from making the biggest, the most terrible mistake of my life? Harry, I swear, I don't know where you get your ideas sometimes. And, by the by, you don't look very good. Why don't you just nip off upstairs and I'll have Pinch order a bath for you? A shave wouldn't come amiss either. Should I hunt out Pinch?"

Without waiting for an answer, he trotted out of the room, the spring back in his step, leaving his brother behind to wonder aloud as to whether or not the fall off his pony and onto his head Willie had taken at the age of six could have something to do with the boy's current rather scattered mental condition.

Harry wasn't left alone very long, unfortunately for his throbbing head; a few minutes later Mr. Grover Saltaire was announced.

"Good Lord, Harry, you look dreadful!" the dapper young man commented cheerfully enough as he sat himself down in the chair facing the duke's and blighted the poor, suffering man with the dazzling smile that had captured Miss Eugenie Somerville's heart. "You'll never guess where Miss Eugenie Somerville is this morning, Harry. Never.

Go ahead—guess. I dare you. You'll never guess, not in a million years. A billion years!''

Harry lowered his chin onto his cravat and gazed levelly at Mr. Saltaire, mentally jotting a note to have Pinch screen all his future visitors for signs of encroaching insanity. "On her way to Gretna Green with Percy Sau-something, visions of ivy-covered cottages and rosy-cheeked babies dancing in her head?" he offered meanly at last, somehow knowing that Salty was referring to Eugenie but not above getting some of his own back for the man's unnerving cheerfulness.

Salty put out his hands and shook his head—still smiling that blighting smile, damn him. "No, no, Harry, you've got it all wrong. That's Helena who's run off to marry over the anvil. Eugenie explained it all to me in a note just this morning. They played a little trick last night, with my dearest darling Eugenie pretending to be her sister at Lady Hereford's. Wasn't that quite a joke? Even I didn't know her."

"Quite a joke, Salty," Harry agreed tightly, reaching for the nearly empty brandy decanter. "As a matter of fact, I've been sitting here laughing out loud about it nearly the whole night long."

Salty puckered up his forehead, which did nothing to mar his near-feminine, fuzzy-cheeked blond beauty—and visibly less to improve his never-sterling intelligence. "You have? My goodness, I hadn't thought about that before. I've just realized, Harry, you won't look quite the hero once this gets out, will you? I mean, letting your ward slip away like that, from right beneath your nose. There might be those who would even say you urged her toward such an obvious misalliance in order to revenge yourself on her papa—not that I believe it for a minute, because Eugenie has told me how truly decent you've been to her—all things considered, that is. There was that contretemps about the gloves, if I recall correctly."

Salty took his bottom lip between his teeth. "Letting the chit toddle off to Gretna, and not so much as pretending to take up the chase? That is a bit much, old son."

Harry pondered whether it would prove worth his effort to brain Salty with the decanter, then decided that it most probably would not. "No one will be any the wiser that Helena eloped, if the child has the belated good sense to return to Portman Square with her groom—which I'm convinced is precisely what they will do, considering the fact that neither of them has a feather to fly with, without Helena's portion, which I, for my sins, have agreed to furnish. I'll put a small announcement in the papers in a few days, saying something about how they were childhood sweethearts and were wedded quietly from some nonexistent aunt's house in Cornwall or some other ungodly place no one would ever think to visit."

Harry took a sip of brandy, happy with the story he had made up as he went along, even though he wasn't quite sure why he thought he owed Salty an explanation. He liked the fellow well enough, he supposed, but both Grover and Sir Roderick were more in the way of acquaintances than friends, and now he was no longer sure if he even liked either one of them. Especially Roddy, he decided meanly, taking another sip of brandy.

A small silence descended on the study as Harry became lost in his own thoughts and Salty waded through all that had been said, vaguely aware that he still hadn't told Harry something of the greatest importance. "I have it now!" he exclaimed at last, jarring Harry's head back with the sheer exuberance of his exclamation. "You haven't guessed yet, Harry." Salty hopped up from the chair.

Harry expelled a deep sigh, wishing himself, if not Salty, at the other end of the earth. "I haven't guessed what yet? Oh, yes. Miss Eugenie Somerville's whereabouts, wasn't it? Please, Salty, I beg you not to keep me in suspense another moment," he said, his tone one of patent disinterest that was not totally lost on Grover. "Tell me the whole, not that I believe you would leave anything out—not a single word. You run with Roddy a lot these days, don't you, Salty?"

Grover pouted, not liking the duke's lack of interest in what, to him, was the most wonderful thing to happen since he had turned five-and-twenty and had at last learned to whistle through his teeth like a coachy. "Eugenie is visiting with dearest Mama at the almshouse!"

Harry, remembering something Trixy had said just last night about believing the way to Mrs. Saltaire's heart lay in Eugenie's shared love of "causes," once more found himself unable to resist temptation. "Your mother lives in an almshouse? Strange, I had always thought you kept a house in Brook Street."

"No, no, no," Salty hastened to explain, "Mama admires good works most excessively, and when Miss Stourbridge sent a note round this morning, tucked in with Eugenie's, hinting that Eugenie shares many of Mama's concerns for the wretched poor, and after I ran to Mama and told her the same things, Mama immediately decided to take Eugenie up with her on her rounds, to test her, I suppose, although there won't be any problem there, as Eugenie is always lamenting the sad fate of the downtrodden, and all that drivel.

"This afternoon they're visiting a home for pregnant prostitutes who have come to see the error of their ways. Isn't that just the grandest thing you've ever heard? And to think—just yesterday Mama told me she loathed Eugenie and threatened to cut me off without a shilling if I mentioned her name at table again—not that she really would, because I'm her only child, you know, and she fairly dotes on me."

"Yes, indeed. How, um, gratifying—all of what you said," Harry murmured softly. Eugenie and Mrs. Saltaire were actually going to visit a household of light-o'-loves? A young, unmarried, innocent girl? She'd probably faint dead away on the doorstep! Was Salty out of his mind, to allow this to happen?

Harry was torn between the desire to laugh out loud at Salty's obvious delight and giving in to the urge to seek Trixy out and gift her with a pithy sermon meant to point out the pitfalls inherent in attempting to make up for one mistake by rushing headlong into committing another.

"Yes, it was a brilliant stroke, Harry," Salty went on happily, oblivious of Harry's dark thoughts. "Mama set me down here and took up Eugenie, and the two of them drove off, Eugenie already in Mama's good graces because the dogs liked her on sight."

"The . . . the dogs?" Harry was suddenly quite tired, and could think of nothing save getting himself upstairs and into a nice soft bed. "I've missed something, haven't I, Salty? What dogs? They're not pregnant, are they?"

Instantly repenting the questions, Harry held out a hand to stop Salty's sure-to-be-lengthy as well as stupefyingly boring explanation. "I don't wish to appear rude, Salty, but it has been a long night, what with Helena's defection and all. Would you mind terribly if I left you now? You can wait for Eugenie's return in the drawing room with Lady Amelia and Miss Stourbridge, who, I am sure, will be more than delighted to share in your joy."

Salty rushed over to the duke and all but pushed him back into his chair. "No, no! You can't leave now! I haven't asked for Eugenie's hand in marriage yet, and I must have her, Harry—truly I must!"

Harry pointedly removed Salty's hands from the sleeves of his coat. "Permission granted, Salty, and with my most grateful thanks," he allowed brusquely. "We'll discuss her portion another time, if you don't mind."

Mr. Saltaire stood up very straight. "That's it? That's all? Don't you want to know if I love her? If I'll cherish her above all else? If I'd lay down my very life to protect her?"

"No," Harry replied baldly, "I don't. I most especially don't wish to hear anything about your great passion for the chit. As a matter of fact, I don't think I care what you do with her, so long as you promise to take her away. I've done enough penance, I think, for daring to try to revenge myself on Myles Somerville. I need a rest."

But Mr. Saltaire wasn't quite done. Grabbing at Harry's hand, he proceeded to pump it up and down with both of his, launching himself into a lengthy speech about how he would be willing to contribute toward an allowance for Helena and her dancing-master husband, and would even go so far as to allow the eloped couple to live under his roof until such time as Eugenie, that dear, loving sister, could be convinced that they should be able to exist on their own.

Thinking that Salty had just blindly condemned himself to a lifetime living cheek by jowl with both twins—and some primping, posturing dancing master—Harry once more gave his blessing to the man and, at long last, convinced him to join Lady Amelia and Trixy in the drawing room or wherever it was that the ladies might be congregating at that particular moment.

It was just as he was making for the doorway that led to the rear of the house and the servants' stair-case—thinking it might then be possible to make his escape to his chamber without encountering his aunt or Trixy—that he was halted in his tracks by the sound of Sir Roderick Hilliard's hearty greeting.

"Just been nattering quite happily this half-hour with your aunt, Harry, waiting for Salty to say his piece," Sir Roderick imparted casually, sitting himself down in the chair recently vacated by Mr. Saltaire and crossing his legs one over the other as if settling in for a lengthy coze—with Sir Roderick there existed no such thing as a brief chat.

"I saw him just now in the hallway, grinning fit to burst. I worried for a moment, I have to own it, believing he might fall on my neck and kiss me! Good of you to give your blessing to his suit, you know. How does it feel, at your age, to be acting the father? I should think it depressing myself, although it might be fun to watch some suitor squirm while I grilled him about his prospects. Well, you won't have that with me, will you, for you know how deep in the pocket I am. And I'm not cheeseparing either, you know that too. I'll not be stingy with her, or keep her on a strict allowance the way you've done. Oh, yes, I've heard about the tantrum you threw over a few paltry modiste bills. I say, Harry, are you going to sit down, or must I do all my pleading to your back?"

Harry, who had taken up a resigned position leaning against the mantelpiece, turned to look at Sir Roderick. "Are you asking me for permission to court Miss Stourbridge?" he asked at last, wondering how low he would have to sink before he would be allowed to drown in his own misery. "I hardly think—"

"No, no, no, Harry!" Sir Roderick interrupted, rising. "Mustn't think, my good man—it's too wearying. Just say yes, won't you? This is no surprise to you, I'm sure, as I've been running tame here in Portman Square ever since first clapping eyes on Trixy. She's old enough not to need your permission—and please don't tell her I said that, as you know how uppity ladies can be about their ages—not that I believe it usual to ask an employer for permission, but she holds rather a strange position in this household, you know. Lady Amelia treats her like a daughter, and you have allowed her to go about in society, dancing and all, and let her get rigged out fine as ninepence at your expense into the bargain, for which I'd be happy to recompense you if that sticks in your craw. The way I figure it, Harry, Trixy's as much your ward as those twins of yours, so I should think it only civil of me to ask you for her hand."

Harry—who had become so used to being considered a closefisted miser, thanks to one brief sermon about gloves, that the label no longer bothered him—immediately felt himself gripped in the saw-toothed jaws of a dilemma. Should he tell Sir Roderick what he knew about Trixy, breaking the besotted man's heart—and possibly earning himself a fist to the jaw—or should he keep silent, allowing the man, who was full-grown and old enough to make his own mistakes, to topple into matrimony with a woman who would stoop to blackmail, not to mention allowing men to kiss her in her private chamber?

And if he did tell Sir Roderick the truth about Trixy, and if the man did then cry off, what would happen to Trixy? Would she retire to some seaside cottage at the end of the Season, as she said she wished to do, to live out the rest of her life on the allowance that was the booty of her blackmailing scheme—so that he would be constantly reminded of her yet would never see her again, hear her again, touch her again? Was that the fate he wanted for her, just so he could know that no other man had what he couldn't have?

And would that be fair to Trixy? Perhaps she really loved Roddy. Perhaps the two of them would marry, have a half-dozen children, and live happily ever after. Harry winced involuntarily at the thought.

"Roddy," he began, not really knowing what he would say, "how well do you know Trixy? I mean, really know Trixy?"

Sir Roderick relaxed into the chair again, stroking his small beard. "Oh, so you do intend to grill me like some doting father. Salty didn't have it half so bad, but then, I already sensed that you don't much care what happens to the Somerville chits as long as they're safely out of your house as soon as possible," he said, then sighed. "Very well, Harry. I'll tell you what I know.

"I know that Trixy's beloved schoolteacher father is dead. I know that she has had to support herself for several years by hiring herself out as a companion to wigeons like the Somerville twins. I know that she is extremely keen about books and history and politics and all that sort of drivel—even talks French and a little Greek, not that I can do more than take her word for that, seeing as how I don't know those languages. She's a graceful dancer, has a lovely singing voice—or, rather, humming voice, for she vows she doesn't sing all that well—dislikes beetroot, looks best in yellows and greens, and is the kindest, sweetest, most gentle creature on the face of the earth. Is that enough, or must I go on?"

Harry's hands had drawn up into tight fists as a pain he knew was part guilt, part genuine heartache, grew in his chest. "You have my permission to ask for Miss Stourbridge's hand, Roddy," he said softly, turning his back to the man, knowing that Sir Roderick had told him things about Trixy that he, who believed himself more than half in love with her, did not know.

"Good Old Harry!" Sir Roderick exploded, crossing the room quickly to clap the duke heavily on the back. "I knew you wouldn't let me down. And to think I accused you of being in love with her yourself! Now . . . I have your permission. Do I have your good wishes and blessing as well?"

Harry looked at his friend out of the corners of his eyes. "My blessing? Don't push me, Roddy," he warned from between clenched teeth before all but stomping from the room, leaving a confused but blissful Sir Roderick behind to wonder if his new breeches were up to the task of allowing him to get down on one knee.

18

HARRY HAD NO IDEA how he was going to get through the next several hours—or the next fifty years, for that matter.

He had all but raced up to his rooms after running out on Sir Roderick. He had allowed himself to be shaved, then had washed quickly at the basin and just as swiftly changed into fresh clothing before dismissing his valet and collapsing into a wing chair beside the cold fireplace, his long legs sprawled out in front of him as he waited in galloping dread for the inevitable summons from his aunt.

His mind was full of jumbled thoughts, none of them holding so much as a thimbleful of comfort. He would have to go downstairs, of course. He would have to offer his congratulations to Sir Roderick and his best wishes to Trixy. He would, as the head of the household, be forced to order a toast drunk to the newly betrothed couple.

He held up his right hand, cradling an imaginary goblet. "To Sir Roderick Hilliard and his lovely

Beatrice I offer an old Irish toast: 'May the sons of your sons smile up in your faces.' " His hand fell into his lap. "I can't do it," he mumbled morosely into his cravat. "I just can't do it."

No other hands save his should be allowed to twine themselves through Trixy's glorious red hair. No other lips should be permitted to taste the sweetness of her soft rosy mouth. No nose save his should smell her jasmine perfume, no other eyes should ever see her lovely, lovable form, or watch her face as she looked up from the mattress, the true wonder of love as it is expressed between two people who cherish each other becoming known to her for the first time.

Harry had told her that he wanted her. He had insulted her with his offer that she become his mistress—a blunder for which he would curse himself into his dotage. But no matter how he had tried to bungle it, Trixy did care for him. He was sure of it. As a matter of fact, if it hadn't been for that miserable Irish maid interrupting them last night with her incoherent blithering and homespun advice, Trixy might be his right now, rather than Sir Roderick's.

"Irish blessing my foot!" he exploded, rising from his chair. "What I really could use now is a good Irish curse!"

He walked to the window that gave onto the square and looked out, suddenly hit with another thought. What if Sir Roderick, who had believed it necessary to ask him for Trixy's hand, also thought it would be following the conventions to have Harry give the bride away? Harry made a fist of his right hand and plowed it into the wall beside the window, nearly crippling himself.

The eloquent stream of curses that followed this unfortunate direction of temper was abruptly cut off as he saw Sir Roderick leave the house, the man's dragging steps and downcast head sending a thrill of hope slicing through Harry's body with the white-hot heat of a lightning bolt.

"She's turned the jabbering magpie down!" he announced to the empty room. "She had everything to gain and nothing to lose, yet that wonderful minx has bloody well turned Roddy down, bless his poor broken heart! Trixy does love me! She must!"

He whirled about, making it halfway to the door before he realized that it wouldn't do to go haring off downstairs until he could wipe the inane grin from his face. After all, it wouldn't be prudent to look too smug, or else Trixy—the adorable sweetheart!—might feel the need to put him through a few more hoops before giving in to the inevitable.

But wait a minute. Trixy had turned down Sir Roderick's suit. That didn't mean she was ready to accept his, did it? The thought gave Harry pause— but only a momentary one. He didn't know when he had decided that marriage to Trixy was the only answer. Perhaps talk of the wedded state from two different gentlemen this morning in his study had got his mind to thinking along such lines.

But that was of no importance. All he really needed to know was that nothing short of marriage to Trixy would rescue him from the depths of despair such as he had been experiencing from the moment Sir Roderick had entered the study.

She was a blackmailer? Harry gave a toss of his head as he checked his appearance in the mirror. What of it? She could be a murderer, a thief, a spy—it didn't matter! He didn't know why he loved her, he didn't know when he had fallen in love with her. All he knew, all he wanted to know, was when he could have her to himself, away from twins and brothers and aunts and the rest of the world.

He leaned forward, inspecting his chin for any signs that his ill humor might have encouraged his valet to rush his morning shave, giving himself yet another moment to collect his thoughts.

"Harry?" called a small nervous voice from the doorway behind him.

It was Trixy. Trixy, here, in his bedchamber. Some benevolent god must be smiling on him. Harry's hand stilled in the action of smoothing his cravat and he slowly turned to face her. "Trixy," he said, amazing himself with the level tone of his voice. "Is something wrong?"

She came more fully into the chamber, closing the door to the hallway behind her. "Wrong?" she asked, her gaze idly wandering over the furnishings, avoiding his. "Whatever could be wrong?"

"Nothing, I suppose, although you must admit it's odd that you are here in my rooms."

She shrugged her slim shoulders. "No odder than having you in mine last night, I should think. We passed beyond the conventions some time ago, Harry."

Harry watched as she moved slowly about the room, lifting a figurine to hold it to the light, straightening the brocade runner that rested upon a nearby table, picking up a book that had been lying open on its spine and reading the title.

She looked wonderful, the golden highlights in her red hair glowing warmly as she passed through a shaft of dusty late-morning sunlight streaming through the window onto the carpet, the book still in her hand. She also, he noted with no small satisfaction, appeared to be more than a little on edge. That boded well for him, he was sure.

"Has there been any word from Helena and her prancing master?" he asked randomly when the silence in the room began to undermine his confidence.

She shook her head, and walked on, nearing the bed before she belatedly saw her error and turned away. "But you may be somewhat comforted to learn that Eugenie is well on her way to becoming a much-beloved daughter-in-law to Mrs. Saltaire. Salty just received a note from his mother summoning him home immediately to share an intimate luncheon with her and 'dearest Eugenie.'"

Harry, who had been so sure of himself just a few minutes previously, was curiously pleased by the chance to talk of other things while his courage, formerly so strong, had some time to rebuild itself. "Salty has offered to share his country house with Helena and her Frenchman until they can settle themselves—which probably means he will have the two of them and their inevitable multitude of children underfoot forever—and he even promised to provide half Helena's allowance as well. It's amazing what love will do to a man's common sense, isn't it?"

Trixy's head came up, and the book—a dull tome recounting the founding of Rome that he had given up on a week ago—snapped shut. "Which do you believe comes first, then, Harry—love for a woman, or the loss of a man's common sense? Or is one necessary to the other? And if a man must first lose his common sense, how can he be sure what he feels for the woman is really love, and not infatuation, or attraction, or even lust?"

"You're upset," he said, wincing at his own understatement. He looked deeply into her eyes, seeing that they held a great pain. "It's Roddy, isn't it? You turned him down."

Trixy's eyes flashed green ice and he knew he had blundered again. "Yes, I turned him down—which probably has shocked you, since you were so sure I'd marry him in order to gain myself a wealthy husband—but no, it's not Roddy that has me upset. It's you, Harry—you big idiot!" And with that said, she turned to leave the room.

"Wait a minute!" Harry commanded, grabbing her upper arm, which earned him another searing look. He let go of her arm as if her skin gave off an unbearable heat and, inclining his head slightly, murmured, "I'm sorry, Trixy. Let me rephrase that. Please . . . stay a moment. We have to talk."

Trixy nodded, not saying anything, for she could not trust her voice, and stood waiting for him to speak. She had come to his chambers only to tell him about Eugenie and to inform him, because he had been the one to give his permission for the match, that she had turned down Sir Roderick's plea for her hand. No, that wasn't quite true, and she knew it.

She had boldly come here to this man's private rooms to watch his face while she told him she had turned down Sir Roderick. She had to watch, she had to know how the news would affect him, if it affected him at all. His response—or, as it pained her to realize, the lack of it—had put her on the brink of tears and she wanted nothing more than to retire to her room and weep.

"What do you want to talk about, Harry?" she asked when he made no move to speak, but just stood there, his hand still outstretched, looking down at her with a most strange, unreadable expression on his face. "I'm not supposed to be in here, and Lady Amelia may be looking for me."

Harry continued to stare at her, struggling to find the right words, but her proximity—especially when he had just thought he'd lost her—was doing strange things to him. Talk? They had no need of talk. She was here. He was here. They were together, where they belonged. And this time he wasn't going to let her get away.

His hand reached out to clasp her waist, and he pulled her to him, having decided to let his actions speak for him once again. Their lips met in an explosion of mutual passion that had them clinging tightly to each other so that they could maintain their physical if not their mental balance.

For neither of them was thinking clearly. They were reacting to the moment, and to the hunger for each other, which had been denied when Lacy had interrupted them last night in Trixy's room and had doubled in force, then redoubled, with each hour that had passed since then.

It was Harry who ended the kiss, reluctantly, and

all but gasping for breath. He whispered hoarsely into Trixy's ear, "Marry me, sweetings. Please."

She rested her head on his shoulder, her face turned away from his as her fingertips curled into his upper arms. Now she knew what she wanted to know—had hoped to learn—for all the good it would do her.

"I can't, Harry," she said quietly, her voice catching on a sob. "That . . . that's why I came to see you in private—to tell you that I can't marry you. And to tell you that I'll be leaving as soon as Eugenie can be settled."

Harry frowned in confusion. "You . . . you knew I'd ask you to marry me? How?" He didn't even bother addressing her notion of leaving him, for he wasn't going to allow any such thing.

She bit her bottom lip for a moment, then told him, "Roddy told me, of course. When I refused his suit, he told me how you had acted when he asked if he could propose to me. He said he had thought the same thing once or twice before and dismissed it, but now it was as plain to him as the nose on Prinny's face that you wanted me for yourself. But I have to admit it—until this moment I wasn't really convinced you wanted to marry me. I . . . I just knew you wanted me."

Harry took out his handkerchief and handed it to Trixy so that she could wipe her streaming eyes. "You're remembering my brutish proposition, aren't you? I could kick myself every time I think of how arrogant that was, and how much I hurt you. But that was when I thought of you as nothing more than a desirable but devious blackmailer. Now it's different. Now I love you, Trixy."

Trixy reached out to trace her fingertips down the clean line of Harry's jaw. "No, Harry, I don't think so. The only reason I'm here at all is that I tried to blackmail you. I foisted Myles Somerville's dullard daughters on you, causing you no end of expense and trouble, and demanded payment from you to keep me silent about Willie's kidnap scheme. Willie has told me of your feelings about right and wrong. You'd remember that in time, whenever we argued, which would probably be often. You'd grow to hate me in the end."

Harry felt a flash of righteous anger slam through him and pushed her hand away. "What sort of villain do you think I am, woman, that I would ever do anything so base, so crass?"

Trixy put out a hand to touch him. "Harry, please—"

"No!" he exploded, losing his temper—most probably owing to a combination of his injured feelings, his unsated desire, and his lack of sleep. "Why don't you just tell the truth, Trixy, and not try to fob me off with lame excuses? You don't love me. You may want me, but you don't love me. Tell me, when you leave, will you still be going to the cottage you'll rent with the allowance you've demanded from me? You do still intend to accept the cottage and allowance I once denied you and then offered back again with both hands—not that I shall ever be invited to visit you there."

Trixy, her stubborn chin thrust out, countered, "Would it make you happier if I rejected the money and was forced to sleep beneath the hedgerows? It's a strange sort of love you bear me, your grace."

Trixy was dying inside, but she wouldn't—

couldn't—let Harry see that. She loved him so much that she thought her heart would break, but she couldn't marry him, and for exactly the reasons she had given him. Perhaps he honestly believed he could live with the thought that his wife was a common blackmailer, but she knew that she couldn't.

All she could do now was brazen it out, keep him angry with her and, much as it pained her, take advantage of his "allowance" so that she could get as far from London as a stagecoach would take her. Once she was settled, she would find employment and repay him, but for now she did need the money. Myles Somerville hadn't paid her in months, and she had used her last quarter's wages to help feed the twins.

But Harry couldn't know any of this. He could only look at her, see the resolution in her green eyes, and take it for greed. "You stupid woman," he said condemningly, turning away from her. "You could have had it all, been my duchess, but you would prefer to cavort shamelessly with Roddy and me, yet maintain your independence, while still planning to bleed me dry with your blackmail. Very well, madam, have it your way. All in all, I'd say you've earned it!"

"Oh, Harry," Trixy said on a sob, reaching out to him, but he had already turned away, and she restrained herself, knowing it was better this way. She would see out the Season, until Eugenie and Helena were safely settled, and then be on her way. It was the only solution.

She was nearing the door when it burst open,

slamming back against the wall. Willie raced into the room panting and looking as if he had just run a very long race. "Trixy! What are you doing in here? Is that proper? I don't think that's proper. Oh, never mind. It doesn't matter. Harry, you'll never guess!"

Harry rubbed a hand across his weary, somewhat moist eyes. "No, William, I'm quite convinced that I won't. My guesses have been rather wide of the mark lately."

"Well, never mind, Harry, that's all right, since you'd never guess anyway, and this is just too important to wait. It's Somerville, Harry. Andy and I just saw him at the bottom of Bond Street, strutting about just like he belonged there. Are you going to go down there and call him out? I'll be your second, Harry, if you'll let me."

"Harry . . ." Trixy began as the duke's spine straightened and he started for the door at a near-run. "Harry, no—don't do this!"

But Harry wasn't listening. He was in just the proper sort of careless, murderous mood to confront Myles Somerville, and damn the consequences!

19

BY NIGHTFALL the duke had returned to Portman Square, three parts exhausted and perilously near the end of his emotional tether. Myles Somerville, if indeed that was who Andy and Willie had seen at the bottom of Bond Street, had gone to ground, and Harry hadn't been successful in uncovering so much as a single lead to the man's whereabouts.

But that didn't really matter, for now Harry had a purpose in life, something to keep his mind off his troubles with Trixy. He would have Pinch find him something to eat, get himself a few much-needed hours of sleep, and then take up the chase once more. Redecorating the slickly handsome Myles Somerville's face with the swift, violent application of his fists would go a long way toward making Harry feel better. A long way, but not all the way. Only Trixy held the power to heal him totally.

As he made for the staircase, his aunt walked out into the foyer and exclaimed, "We have been wondering where you went flying off to, nephew.

Trixy has been extremely secretive as to your whereabouts—going out on her own for a while herself this afternoon with naught but that Lacy woman to attend her—and because we had considered quizzing young William to be a total waste of our effort, we had resigned ourselves to waiting for you to find your way home. But that is no matter anymore, is it, for you are home now, and there has been a most distressing, unlooked-for development in the past hour that requires your immediate attention."

"Not now, Aunt," Harry pleaded wearily, his right foot already on the first step. "I think I've had about enough distressing developments for one day. If Helena has returned, with or sans one husband, feed her, or them, and put them to bed. If Eugenie has returned with a dog, do the same with them. However, if she has returned with a raddled, reformed, pregnant prostitute in tow . . . well, just don't tell me about it, all right? Where is Pinch?"

"We are not amused, nephew," Lady Amelia protested with a pout that was less queenly than aggrieved. "Oh, good, here's Pinch now. He'll explain for us," she said more cheerfully, tugging at the butler's arm as he approached from the direction of the drawing room, "won't you, Pinch?"

Harry looked at the butler, whose facial expression at that moment could most readily be described by the mere recitation of the butler's name, and motioned for the man to speak.

"Begging your pardon, your grace," the butler began, bowing, "but it would appear we have a small upset in the drawing room."

"A small upset," the duke repeated. "What's it's name?" he asked, rubbing a hand across his blood-shot eyes, for running down a list of the current inhabitants of Portman Square capable of causing "a small upset" could take some time.

"Myles Somerville, sir," Pinch informed his master, hastening to add, "He came knocking on the front door an hour past, demanding his daughters be brought out immediately. I didn't quite know what to do with him, so I put him in the drawing room. But it's not so bad as it sounds, your grace. Young Master Willie and Master Andrew got him all trussed up right quick, so's he won't go anywhere."

This last piece of information was delivered to the duke's back, as Harry was already on his way to the drawing room, Lady Amelia following along in his wake, admonishing her nephew to promise her he would not go into a taking.

Harry threw open the double doors to the drawing room so that they slammed back loudly against the wall, causing the three male heads in the room to turn in the direction of the sound.

"Sir! Lookee what we got!" This jovial exclamation came from Andy, who had been interrupted as he was perched, birdlike, on the arm of a chair, pulling faces at the captive.

"Good Old Harry!" Willie called out, grinning widely as he advanced on the duke, as if expecting, like some faithful hound, to be patted on the head for his good behavior. "Happy birthday a month early, my dearest brother. How do you like my gift? I've even got it all tied up in ribbons for you!"

"Mmmfff, mmmfff," Myles Somerville grunted as he strained against the half-dozen silken drapery cords that anchored him to a blue brocade arm-chair, his powers of speech limited, thanks to the white handkerchief—bearing a neatly mono-grammed W on one corner—stuffed halfway into his mouth.

"My God," Harry remarked, taking in the scene, "it is true." He walked fully into the room, his stare directed at his nemesis. "William, was Pinch right in saying that Somerville just waltzed in here demanding the twins? It seems impossible to me that any one man could be that stupid." He walked clear around the tied-up man, flicking the bonds encasing the man's upper arms with one finger. "It fairly boggles the mind."

"What are you going to do with him, Harry?" Willie asked, hopping about on one foot in his excitement. "Are you going to duel, or are you going to take a horsewhip to him? Gentlemen don't really duel with scoundrels, do they? They wouldn't dirty their hands. They just horsewhip them. Isn't that right, Harry? Andy says so, and he read about it in a book."

The duke shook his head, his humor much improved by the woebegone sight before his eyes. "So many surprises in one day, William," he murmured softly, still looking at the twins' errant father. "First Somerville's reappearance, and now you tell me Andrew here has read a book. His parents would absolutely burst with pride if they should learn of it."

Unbeknownst to Harry, Trixy had entered the

drawing room, deliberately remaining silent until she could assure herself that Harry wasn't about to do something foolish in his need to revenge himself upon any convenient target for the unending chaos that had lately become his life. His remark about Andy comforted her greatly and she remained where she was, awaiting further developments.

The duke bent and removed the gag, watching impassively as Somerville tentatively exercised his jaw a time or two and ran his tongue around his dry lips in an attempt to moisten them. "Where are my daughters, you scoundrel?" were the man's first words once he had satisfied himself that he had regained control of his own mouth. "If you've ruined them, as God is my judge, I'll have your liver and lights for the evil deed. I swear it!"

"Perhaps you should have thought of that before you ran off, Somerville," Harry offered silkily, "leaving two such adorable innocents to my tender mercies."

Somerville so strained against his bonds that Willie, who still held a tender spot in his heart for Helena, was moved to reassure their obviously distraught, repentant sire. Putting a comforting hand on the man's shoulder, he said, "Harry's just jesting, Somerville. He hasn't harmed a hair on their heads. As a matter of fact, he gave them both a cupboard full of fancy clothes and a really first-rate ball so's he could pop them off. Didn't he, Andy?"

"Right you are, Willie," Andy answered, nodding emphatically, "and even if Helena did run off to

Gretna with that foolish dancing master, Eugenie landed upright with that Salty fellow she just got herself betrothed to this very day. One happy ending outta two ain't so shabby, right?"

As Andy's words penetrated Somerville's brain, he threw back his head and let out a mighty roar reminiscent of a lion whose paw has been snared in a trap. "You can't do this to me! I had buyers for the both of them in Dublin—at twenty thousand pounds apiece! I'm ruined! Ruined, do you hear me!"

"We most certainly do," Harry answered, beginning to feel much better, "although I don't believe we really need to hear you anymore now that we know what caused you to lose your fear of me to the point that you would dare to come knocking at my door. William, do the world a favor and replace the gag."

Willie did as his brother directed—rather ungently, it must be added—then ran across the room to stand in front of Trixy. "You were right all along, Trixy," he said, marveling at both her insightful intelligence and Somerville's depravity. "You were right to do what you did, and even if things didn't work out between Helena and me—seeing as how I don't think I really want to wed as yet and was just suffering from calf love, like Andy told me— she and Eugenie have you to thank for saving them from what that terrible man planned for them."

"Thank you, Willie," Trixy said, retrieving the hand the boy had been in danger of ripping off by way of his enthusiastic shaking of that appendage, "but I only took advantage of an opportunity with which you and Andy, in your innocence, provided me."

"That's true enough," Andy piped up, sensing yet another opportunity—this time one whose benefits he could immediately reap. "We're heroes, Willie, do you know that? Actually, I'm the real hero, for the whole kidnap scheme was my plan, as you recall."

Willie's eyes narrowed as he stomped across the floor to go chin to chin with his bosom chum. "Your idea, Andy? Well, if that don't just beat the Dutch! Who was it what brought the sack and the mallet and arranged for the extra carriage? Answer me that, you miserable—"

"Boys, boys," Harry interrupted, sensing the eminent outbreak of fisticuffs in his drawing room while there was still so much left unsettled, "I think we can save this particular discussion for another time. Right now, we must consider what to do with Somerville here, as I don't look forward to having him become a permanent fixture of this room. Any ideas?"

Somerville, his mouth stuffed full of handkerchief once more, looked apprehensively from one youth to the other, obviously reluctant to have his fate decided by either of them.

"Strip him, horsewhip him, and throw him out into the square!" Willie shouted, instantly diverted. "I'll send Pinch round to the stables for a whip while you slip out of your jacket, Harry, so that you can take a good wide swing."

"Hand the rascal over to a press-gang and have him launched to China," Andy, never at a loss for imagination, suggested hard on the completion of Willie's bloodthirsty solution.

Trixy sighed and gave up her stance at the edge of the room to walk directly up to Somerville. "There's no need for anything quite so drastic," she said, looking down at the man, who had begun to perspire freely in the cool room. "Once Mr. Somerville hears what I have to say, I would imagine he will be most happy to sign on as a crewman sailing to China, or anywhere else for that matter, without further delay."

Lady Amelia, who had been taking in the entire scene from the doorway, giggled girlishly and began to applaud. "We knew it, nephew, we just knew it! Trixy is so quick, so inventive. We just knew she would be the one to bring everything right. We're ever so glad you chose her, Harry. Ever so glad."

Harry closed his eyes and began counting to ten. Someday he was going to have to sit down and have a heartfelt chat with his aunt about just where she had gotten this long-standing misconception of hers concerning his intentions toward Trixy, not that he disagreed with it. But not now. Not while Trixy was standing so majestically over Myles Somerville as that formerly arrogant man literally quivered in his highly polished Hessians.

"What have you done, Trixy?" the duke asked, coming up behind her to place a hand on her waist. "I know you've done something, mostly because I know you. Besides, Aunt Amelia already informed me that you went out this afternoon."

Trixy closed her eyes a moment, fighting the urge to lean against Harry's strength one last time before once more damning herself out of her own mouth. She didn't want to do it, but she could see no other way to save Harry from ending up on the wrong side of a dueling pistol, for no matter how inventive Willie and Andy's plans, it was imperative to her that Somerville be routed at once—and for all time.

"Mr. Somerville," she began, forcing her voice to remain calm, "do you by chance remember the music box you gave the twins when you visited them on their last birthday? The particularly gaudy silver one with one leg broken off—so that you couldn't get a good price for it in any of the shops?"

Somerville's eyes widened perceptibly and his shoulders heaved as he strained against his bonds.

"I think you can safely take that as a yes, Trixy," Harry said, his hand pressing more firmly against her spine as he felt her body trembling.

"There was an inscription inside the lid, Mr. Somerville, which you would have known if you had taken the trouble to look," Trixy pressed on doggedly. " 'To my dearest Marianne, from her devoted Oglesby.' It took me some time, but I eventually discovered a man who I was fairly sure was Marianne's devoted Oglesby."

Somerville's physical agitation became so pronounced that Willie had to put out a hand to steady the man's chair, for it was in imminent danger of toppling over backward.

"By some happy coincidence, the man I was looking for was in his office in Whitehall when I went to call this afternoon. Although I did not have an appointment, he was gracious enough to see me after I had his aide take the music box in to him.

He recognized it at once, of course, as the one his—how should I say this?—his very good friend had lost during a robbery at her lodgings last spring."

Harry, who had been turning the name Oglesby over and over in his head, snapped his fingers as the answer hit him. "Oglesby! Of course! Good God, Somerville, were you insane or was it just dumb bad luck that you stumbled upon the man's light-o'-love? I've never heard of this Marianne person, which has to mean that her existence must be considered some sort of state secret. Oglesby may do most of his work behind the scenes, but the man's probably the second-most powerful figure in government today!"

He turned to Trixy, his own thoughts of revenging himself on Somerville erased without regret by the sheer genius of Trixy's brilliant stroke. "Did you tell Oglesby it was Somerville who robbed his paramour? Does he have his men out now, scouring the streets for him? By God, if I know Oglesby, there'll be at least one more quiet beheading in the Tower for the ravens to witness. Come on, Trixy, tell us!"

Trixy opened her mouth to speak, but was forestalled by Andy, who pointed out that Myles Somerville had swooned dead away at the duke's mention of the Tower, and suggested they wait until someone roused the fellow before finishing the story, an idea that suited Trixy quite well, as it had been a very trying day and Harry was standing much too close for comfort. She needed time alone to recover her composure.

Leaving Willie and Andy behind as guards, and

with Lady Amelia retiring to her room to begin planning Eugenie's wedding, now that she was assured that Myles Somerville's reappearance wasn't going to make a mess of things, Trixy allowed Harry to guide her out onto the wrought-iron balcony that overlooked the gardens.

"You can tell me the rest, Trixy," the duke said as they walked. "Did you make Oglesby a gift of Somerville's name so that he could dispose of him discreetly, or are you planning to simply blackmail Somerville into disappearing from his daughters' lives forever?"

Trixy looked up at him, her face white and pinched. "What do you think I did, Harry?"

"That scene back there wasn't easy for you, was it?" Harry questioned soothingly as she pulled herself free of his light hold to lean both hands on the railing. "Were you shaking that much when you first confronted me that night at Glyndevaron? Your voice and expression certainly didn't give you away, but tonight I could feel you trembling through your clothes. I don't think you're really made for a life of crime, even if you do have the wit for it. No, I don't think you're up to another round of blackmail. I imagine Oglesby's agents are already scouring the city for Somerville, with orders to dump him in the Thames."

Trixy's knuckles turned white as she gripped the rail with all her might, not knowing whether to throw herself into Harry's arms for recognizing that she wasn't a hardened blackmailer or to slap his face for suggesting she could blithely hand over a man, even a man so corrupt as Somerville, to be murdered.

In the end her pride won out, for she had already planned her departure from the Glynde mansion and couldn't bear to leave with the one true love of her life once more believing an untruth about her. She turned away from the rail, looked up into the duke's eyes, and said softly, "I didn't go to see Oglesby this afternoon, Harry, although I had taken great pains over the past year to discover Oglesby's probable identity, just in case I should ever need to use it to save the twins, for I knew almost immediately that their father was an evil man.

"I was only bluffing, Harry, making what I hoped was a lucky guess. I couldn't turn any man over to be murdered, even him. If Somerville hadn't believed me, I don't know what I would have done. As it happened, I had guessed right and my bluff worked, so when he wakes up, I imagine Somerville will be more than happy to leave England forever."

Harry was quiet for some moments, digesting the realization that Trixy would have made a good general—or a fantastically successful gamester— then asked, "If you weren't with Oglesby, then where were you? You did go out this afternoon."

Trixy allowed her chin to drop toward her breast. "I was driving about in a smelly hackney with Lacy moaning and groaning and loudly calling on all the angels and saints in alphabetical order the whole while—looking for you, trying to stop you from calling Somerville out and ruining your life."

Harry's smile beamed at her through the gray light of dusk that was descending over the city. "I knew it! You do love me. You love me and I love you, no matter how we seem to scream at each other. Trixy, we have to put an end to this once and for all. Tell me, if I promise to write a thousand times 'I will never get angry and accuse Trixy of being a blackmailer, so help me God,' will you marry me?"

A single tear made its way down Trixy's cheek. "It would never work, Harry. I love you, I really do, but I can never forget that I tried to use you, that I tried to blackmail you."

Harry hadn't expected any other answer, for if he had learned one thing about Trixy, it was that she could be extremely pigheaded, bless her darling heart, so that he immediately reverted to the plan he had formulated during the long hours he had spent fruitlessly combing the city for Somerville.

"All right, Trixy, if you want to be stubborn," he said, his voice deliberately low and gruff, "I guess I have nothing else to do but point out to you that I could have thrown you into jail for what you tried to do to me. Do they still make the women beat hemp in Bridewell, or has that gone by the boards?"

Of all the arguments Trixy had heard and was prepared to hear again, she was taken completely by surprise by Harry's sudden attack. Her head snapped back as she glared openmouthed into his face. "Harry!" she said in shock. "You wouldn't!"

His hands clasped her upper arms as his left foot snaked out to push the door to the drawing room closed. "Are you asking me or telling me, Trixy? But no, of course I wouldn't do any such thing. For a price, that is."

"A price?" she asked, not sure if she liked the smile that was nipping at the corners of the duke's mouth. "What sort of price?"

Harry's head came down as he began nibbling delicately at the tip of Trixy's ear. "Mmmm, you taste good. My price, you ask? Why, I think marriage to me would serve to keep me silent. After all, I would never have my own wife thrown in jail."

Trixy bit her bottom lip as delicious shivers ran down the side of her throat. "Jail or marriage to you? That . . . that's blackmail, Harry," she told him, trying for but failing to inject censure into her tone as her arms came up to encircle his neck.

Harry pulled his head slightly away from hers. "Yes, it is rather like blackmail, isn't it? I must have learned it from you," he remarked, lightly flicking at the tip of her nose with his finger. "How nice of you to recognize my plan so quickly."

"You call that a plan?" Trixy questioned, scoffing. "You'd never drag your brother's name through the mire to hurt me. That's no plan, Harry. I bluffed Somerville, and now you are trying out a bluff of your own. But I'm wise to you, Harry. Your threat to blackmail me is nothing but a farce."

"Exactly," he agreed amicably, sensing that his victory was at hand. "It's a farce. Your plan to blackmail me, although vaguely brilliant, was a farce. My ridiculous offer to set you up as my mistress was a farce, although not very laughable at the time. Why, now that I think on it, every encounter we have had, Miss Stourbridge, has been little more than farcical—except perhaps for a few isolated moments reminiscent of the one we are having now."

His smile faded and a resolute expression crept

into his eyes. "But, be that as it may, my love, your staunch resolve to deny us both what the two of us know we want, simply because you made one small mistake, has forced me to stoop, as it were, to your level. If you are to go through life as a blackmailer, then so shall I. Happily, I might add, since I will be going through that life by your side.

"And so, sweetings, if this plan of mine is a farce, it is the final farce, for my mind is quite made up. Now, which is it to be, Beatrice—jail or marriage to a blackmailer?"

Epilogue

ONCE UPON A TIME IN MAYFAIR, a small, strange land snuggled neatly within the general confines of London, where marriage is most often considered to be either convenient or financially astute, "loyalty" and "fidelity" are words gentlemen usually reserve for their horses and their clubs, and a firstborn son is likely to be the only offspring to resemble its mother's husband, there resided—only during the Season, as they much preferred the quiet of the country or long, leisurely weeks spent aboard their yacht—the Duke and Duchess of Glynde, a couple so disgustingly in harmony with each other that at least one disgruntled peer was overheard to whisper *sotto voce* as the happy pair waltzed by at a ball that, "the man's giving matrimony a bad name."

The duke and duchess had not traveled to London alone, for, no matter what their wishes in the matter might be, they had already learned to their peril that to leave the duke's brother, Lord William, behind at Glyndevaron was courting, if not actually begging for, disaster, since adding another year to his not very considerable age had done nothing to convince Willie that he had any other mission in life save to enjoy it to the top of his bent, and damn the consequences.

Because Willie could not bear to be separated overlong from his closest friend, Andrew Carlisle, the duke and duchess were likewise blessed with that rascally fellow's presence, which greatly explained not only Harry's sometimes eagle-alert expression when the boys were anywhere about but also the raw wood coffin that had been found propped against the front door of the lord high mayor himself one morning after the boys had spent a particularly frisky night on the town.

The very first week Harry and his Trixy were in town, they hosted a small party in honor of Grover Saltaire and his wife, Eugenie, Harry having decided that the best way to get over rough ground was to do it as quickly as possible, as they were bound to run into each other eventually.

In attendance at the dinner party, besides Salty and his bride—and his mother and three particularly ugly pug dogs, of course—was Miss Helena Somerville, still unmarried, as she had returned to Portman Square the same night her father sailed for China, complaining to all who would listen that she had decided against marrying any high-and-mighty Frenchman who thought she should carry his baggage from the stagecoach to the inn at Watford just because he used to be Somebody.

All in all, Helena had been gone from the Glynde mansion for less than twenty-four hours, with most of those hours passing in the company of one Agatha Twitter, who had providentially come along to tap M. Sauveur on the head with her umbrella before taking Helena under her wing. With her reputation—and her stunning good luck—intact, she had suffered no lasting damage from the adventure.

Not that Helena was entering her second Season totally without prospects, for Sir Roderick Hilliard had become her near-constant companion, his appreciation for beauty without the added encumbrances of either intelligence or wit having grown sevenfold over the past year. As a matter of fact, Trixy had already learned that Roddy was planning to propose to Helena before the king's birthday in June, believing that a full twelve months should pass between proposals, just for luck, of course.

Lady Amelia had not made the trip from Glyndevaron this year, much preferring to remain at home to await the arrival of the son of her third cousin, Henrietta, from America. Lady Amelia had every intention of summing up the lad before deciding whether to take on the project of finding him a suitable wife, believing that, having settled Harry so nicely, she had become an expert in the arena of matrimony.

All in all, it must be said that Henry Lyle Augustus Townsend, in the third week of the Season, was the picture of a happy man as he bade Pinch a good night and guided his yawning wife upstairs upon returning from a party that had been graced by none other than Prinny himself.

Trixy, who until a year ago had never dreamed

that she and the heir to the throne of England should ever inhabit the same house, let alone sit at the same dinner table, was blissfully happy, as well as in the very best of looks in a new gown of softest yellow that, unbeknownst to her, Harry was already planning to divest her of the moment the door to their chamber closed behind them.

"Did you see Salty this evening, darling?" Trixy asked as she reached behind her to unclasp the Glynde family diamonds that still served to make her nervous each time she wore them. "He took me aside to tell me that Eugenie is expecting their first child this fall. Isn't that wonderful?"

Harry quickly offered to help her with the clasp, placing a kiss on her bared nape when he was done. "Wonderful indeed, my love. Just what this island needs—another beautiful ninny out to save the world from itself. Salty told me Eugenie and his mother have just set up a haven for repentant pickpockets somewhere in Piccadilly. A school for pickpockets, more likely. Good God, Trixy—what if it's twins? Salty's mother most probably would adore a litter. Why, if Eugenie proves prolific, in twenty years one of them might just be setting up a haven for depraved dukes!"

Turning into his arms, Trixy raised one eyebrow as she smiled up at her husband. "Depraved dukes, Harry? Do you mean to say you've become depraved and I didn't notice? And I thought we had no more secrets from each other. Shame on you."

He reached behind her to begin working on the long row of covered buttons that ran down the back of her gown. "It's only a limited depravity, my pet—and it has a lot to do with what I'd like to do with the glories hiding beneath this gown I wish you were no longer wearing. Why, the way I feel right now, we might just begin trying to balance out the general intelligence of the next generation by providing England with some offspring of our own."

As the gown slipped from her shoulders and her husband lifted her high against his chest, heading unhesitatingly toward the wide tester bed, Trixy buried her head into his shoulder to hide her delighted smile. "Good Old Harry," she complimented him, giggling as she used Willie's favorite name for his brother. "You're always so adept at finding ways to even things out. But just think of it—what if we should end by bringing another enterprising blackmailer into the world?"

Harry considered this possibility for a few moments as he shrugged out of his jacket and shirt, then smiled down at his wife, who was lying comfortably on the coverlet, waiting for him.

"A farce in *three* acts? Personally, my love, considering how we managed to find each other," he said, blowing out the bedside candle before joining his wife on the bed, "I can't think of any more perfect way we could all be assured of living happily ever after."

It must be added here that precisely nine months and six days later, the lustily howling, red-faced, dark-haired Henry Lyle Augustus Townsend II entered the world in the master chamber at Glyndevaron—to be instantly dubbed "Black Harry" by his overjoyed parents, who greatly enjoyed their private joke.